Saved by Mr. Tempting

Deal with consequences

You are mine 1

Rebecca Baker

Copyright 2023
Rebecca Baker
All rights reserved

Sign up for my newsletter and receive a free romance novel:
https://dl.bookfunnel.com/oe2w1m9zxx

Chapter 1

Nate

It was all mine. The office, the building, the company, all in my name. I was having a hard time believing it. Even wandering around the CEO's suite, I couldn't believe my good fortune. My father was out, and I was in. Just like that, I was catapulted to a leadership role and became one of the youngest influential businessmen in the country.

I could call up the presidents of any Fortune 500 company and ask for lunch. They would fall all over themselves to oblige, rolling out the red carpet if I gave any hint of interest. My name was in the *Wall Street Journal*, along with the story of how I made my first million.

It seemed like so long ago, but it was really just ten years. And I was working for my parents, up until the divorce. What my dad lost in the court battle, I gained. My mom turned the entire enterprise over to me, putting me in charge of hundreds of thousands of workers and real estate holdings in all fifty states.

I had the chops to do well. While I wasn't accustomed to the CEO role, I had at least ten years of middle management under my belt. That meant I could politick with the best of them. I knew all the power players in the company, their likes and dislikes, and how to get them on board. The energy in the building was electric. Everyone knew it was my first day, and they were eager to see where I would go with the organization.

I had yet to sit down with all the books to figure out what my dad did wrong. I knew exactly where his mistakes lay, and they weren't with the finances. He was a serial cheater, and it all started right here in this very office.

The desk caught my eye and I frowned. I was sure something nasty happened in that chair and across the surface of the massive walnut slab. It had probably happened many times, with many different women. I didn't want to imagine my dad banging his secretary right where I was trying to eat my lunch. The first thing that was going to go was the desk.

At the moment, though, my mom was sitting cross-legged on top of it, holding one of Dad's credit cards in her manicured hand. She snipped it in two with a pair of scissors, laughing wickedly.

Her hair was dyed pink and teased out with product. She looked a little bit like a 1980s rock star, though I was too young to know which one. She wore bright red lipstick, and her fingernails were a pale green. She was dressed like a hippie in a pair of leggings and a baby doll dress. I had never seen her look so comfortable or so relaxed.

I watched as she picked up another card from the desk and cut that one in half, tossing both halves over her shoulder. Working her way through a small pile of credit cards, she was having fun. I didn't have the heart to share what I suspected the desk had been used for, previous to our arrival. She was all too familiar with Dad's proclivities; I didn't need to throw them back in her face.

My parents had been married for almost forty years, since long before I was born. I don't know how old I was when my mom first learned my dad was cheating on her, but I must have been young. She just hid the pain and didn't say a thing until it all got to be too much for her. Most recently, Dad was caught banging his secretary, Lauren.

That was the final straw. Mom took him to court and won, taking his cash, his car, and his company. He didn't fight her. I think he was embarrassed to be caught, and possibly even ready to retire. It was always his plan to hand the business over to me anyway; this just sped up the process.

I tried to keep an open mind and maintain good relations with both my parents. I didn't approve of what Dad had done, but he was still my dad. Eventually, I might need his help to make some business decision, so it was in my best interests to remain friendly. But Mom was a different story. She was in my life whether I wanted her there or not. She wasn't the type to take no for an answer.

On day one, she installed herself on my father's desk and made a game out of destroying his credit cards. I couldn't get any work done while she was there. At the very least, I couldn't use the desk, and considering what it had been used for, I wanted nothing to do with it.

I stood by the window, looking out over Boston. It was such an old city, with brick buildings and narrow walkways. I loved it the way you can only love a place called home. I'd grown up there, going to a private school downtown and then to Harvard.

Of course, I had been all over the world. My father had a private jet, and when I was a teenager, he was in the habit of taking the family on spontaneous vacations. Come to find out, he was boning the flight attendants, but I didn't know that at the time.

We went to France and Italy, to Canada and even Japan. We didn't stay in any country for more than a few days before flying back, but we saw enough that I had a taste of what the rest of the world was like. I couldn't see myself settling anywhere outside Boston, though. The exorbitant price of living did little to scare me away. I wasn't hurting. I grew up rich and landed on my feet. If anyone could tame this concrete jungle, it was me.

There was a knock on the door.

"Come in!" I called, turning away from my view.

Dad's secretary, Lauren, came in, her arms full of files. She looked at my mother perched atop the desk and frowned. I raised my eyebrows, daring her to comment. She chose discretion, keeping her adulterous mouth shut.

She wasn't sure what to do with her files, and so she hovered awkwardly near the door. I hadn't asked for anything, and I didn't know why she'd brought them. I didn't care. She was the last person I wanted to see. If there was one particular extramarital affair that sparked my mother's ire, it was Lauren. The woman was a secretary. How much more cliché could you get? It was bad enough that my dad was sticking it to women he met overseas, but he fell back on the most overused trope in the book.

Mom didn't look up. She was concentrating on destroying my father's financial lifeline. I was grateful that she didn't seem to mind Lauren's presence. I didn't want to preside over a cat fight on my first day.

"What do you need, Lauren?" I asked.

"These are the Oliver files," she said, holding them out.

I stepped forward, scooping them out of her hands. "Is that everything?"

"I'm organizing the client files so that you'll be able to find things going forward," she replied, straightening up to her full height.

"I didn't ask you to do that." I couldn't help the acidic tone in my voice. I didn't like her, and I didn't approve of what she'd done to my mom. Lauren knew that my father was married. She had met me when I was in college and an intern in the family business. She knew and didn't care, and that was almost worse than what my father did.

Lauren pressed her lips shut. I was making this difficult for her, but I couldn't bring myself to feel bad. She deserved the clipped words and cold shoulder I was throwing her way. She knew she was out the moment I was in, and her desire to pretend to be professional stuck in my throat the wrong way.

"You know this is your last day?" I asked, just to be clear.

"I know," she said. "I just thought I could leave things organized for you."

"There's no need," I replied.

"Fine." She pursed her lips, shaking her hair out defiantly. "I'll clean my desk out and be gone by lunch."

"Good," I said.

"I'll send you your schedule over email," she threw out as she strode from the room.

My schedule? Did I already have meetings to attend? Had I walked right into my father's shoes without a chance to get settled? Was someone waiting outside right now? I poked my head out of my office to look around. There was no one waiting for me other than Lauren.

She looked up from her own desk, a cardboard box settled comfortably on top. I was pleased to see that she was doing exactly as asked. The sooner she was cleaned out and gone from the building, the better I would feel. I didn't want her to leave without explaining her last statement, though.

"You said you were going to email me my schedule?" I walked toward her, taking up residence beside her desk.

She was about to put a stapler in her box but thought better of it. "Yes."

I didn't care about the stapler, but I could tell that it wasn't hers. I grabbed a framed picture of her as a teenager astride a pony and placed it in the box. If she couldn't tell, I was helping her pack.

"Do I have any meetings today?" I asked.

She shot me a hateful glance. "It's not my fault."

"What's not your fault?" I demanded.

"Figure it out for yourself," she snapped, grabbing a potted plant from the corner of her desk and stuffing it into the box.

I countered by picking up a paperweight and dropping it down next to the plant. She held my gaze, her eyes burning with indignation. She ripped a drawer out and scooped up a handful of candy bars, never breaking eye contact.

Tired of that stupid game, I went back to my office. The email with my schedule probably wouldn't show after all. I would just have to figure it out as I went along. I realized that before I worried about what had or hadn't occurred on the office furniture, I would need a secretary.

It would have to be someone who was easy to work with, who was pleasant and intelligent. I wanted someone who would make a good impression on all the clients and managers who came to talk to me, but not someone who would steal the show. And I definitely didn't want anyone who would tempt me into a romantic relationship. I didn't want to follow in my father's footsteps. An office affair was out of the question.

When I hired a secretary, she would be a professional. I would maintain my distance at all times, treating her like a colleague, and nothing more. If we had to work late, we would each stay in our own office and communicate over the intercom. She would definitely keep my schedule and not lord it over me, as if I was incapable of setting an appointment myself.

I was eager to get started, but again, my mother was sitting on my desk. I looked longingly at the computer perched right beside her knee. Maybe I could bring my old desk up here for the time being. That was probably the best course of action. I could work around both my mother and my father, leaving their whole saga for another day. Realizing that I was going to have to take matters into my own hands, I walked out of the office. Past Lauren's desk and down the hall, I retraced my steps to my old office.

One of the VPs was in the room, taking a phone call. I interrupted him, "Hey. I'd like to take this desk with me."

"Of course," he replied without thinking about it.

"I'm short a secretary," I admitted. "Would you get a few folks to move it?"

"Sure thing." He shut his phone and put it in his pocket, following me out into the hall.

"Are you using that office?" I asked.

"I haven't been transferred yet," he replied. "Although it's the best one next to your dad's. I mean yours." He looked sheepish, as if I was going to be upset with him for bringing up my father's name.

"We can put one of the desks from the third floor in there," I said.

"No problem," he agreed.

I walked back to my office to wait for the cavalry. I had a new desk and a new chair coming. All I needed now was a secretary.

Chapter 2

Ava

The line was ginormous, and I was all the way at the end. I wore my best outfit, though how it managed to escape being wrinkled like everything else I owned escaped me. Maybe it was because I kept it in a garment bag on a hook in the back seat of my car, while everything else was piled up on the front seat.

I was living out of my car; that's how low I'd sunk. I tried not to think about it too much. There was no use getting all depressed about my situation. It wasn't always going to be like it was now. All I needed was a job and a few paychecks, and I could rent my own apartment. Things would start looking up, and I could put this entire experience behind me.

It was a little bit scary the first few nights I spent outdoors. I drove around until I found a secluded spot, and then turned off all my lights and locked the doors. It got pretty cold at night, but luckily I had a sleeping bag. I told myself it was like camping. I used to like camping when I was younger. This was just a hiccup in what was otherwise a smooth life.

I grew up in and around Boston. I'd gone to school to become a newscaster. It was part journalism, part on-camera acting, and I got really good grades. I had a good nose for the stories people wanted to hear and a way of explaining complex facts that won me straight As. I was on a path straight to the top when I was interrupted by a hurricane in the form of a man.

I landed a coveted internship at a local media station, beating out a bunch of other students for the opportunity. And I fell in love with a classmate who invited me to move in with him. Thank goodness I bought the car while I was living there. Marcus tried to talk me out of it, telling me that I didn't need to drive around Boston. There was public transportation and most people just walked. There wasn't a lot of good parking, and it would be more expensive to pay for another spot in his apartment building's lot.

I shrugged off all his negativity and picked out the perfect little compact car. I just wanted something that was my own, and at the time I didn't think that I would ever find myself in dire financial straits. The car was just big enough to cart my groceries around and to get me from point A to point B. I had to have a car to do my job, since part of it involved going out into the community to cover the news.

Marcus could only see that extra four hundred per month for a parking spot in one of the most prestigious locations in the city. And I agreed, it was a fortune, but what was I going to do? I loved my little internship, and I didn't think the money mattered.

That was before he kicked me out. At least I had a roof over my head, though, so I was grateful that I'd stood up to him. Then again, if I was a little mousier, I might still have a spot in his bed. Not that I wanted it. *Good riddance,* I told myself. He was a cheat and a liar, and he was seeing other women behind my back, all while telling me that he loved me.

I didn't need him. I would land on my feet real soon. I quit my internship as soon as Marcus kicked me out. Course credit was great, but I needed something to pay the bills. I needed food in my belly and an apartment to go home to at night, in that order. My career as a newscaster would have to wait.

When Marcus first broke things off, I found a job at a local coffee shop. It was a fun environment with all the free coffee I could drink, but it wasn't enough. I needed a real job with benefits and stock options. I needed something I could sink my teeth into, something that would give me at least fifty or sixty thousand a year. The only thing I could think of that would provide that much money was executive secretary.

Of course, there were other, more lucrative jobs that you could get without a master's degree, but I was too shy to dance on tables. I didn't have the chops to be a stockbroker, and I couldn't sell anything to anyone. My bachelor's degree was nearly worthless without practical experience. And besides, the job market was saturated with people who had better, more impressive resumes.

I shifted on my feet, eager to see if the line was moving up ahead. There were at least twenty other candidates stretching from the door of the massive office building out to the street. I was one of the last, which was fine. I was optimistic enough to think that they would give us all an equal shot. All I had to do was impress the hiring manager and I was sure to get in. None of the rest of the women had what I had: the strength of character and presence of mind to dedicate their every waking moment to the job. Who was I kidding? None of the rest of them were as desperate as I was. I knew for a fact that at least ninety percent of the other candidates had homes and bathrooms with running water.

I tried not to think about the "bath" I'd taken earlier that day, rubbing antiseptic wipes down my arms and across my stomach. I still smelled faintly of lemon, but that was covered up by the lilac of my deodorant.

It was a long shot, but I knew that I could do the job as advertised if they just gave me a chance. I was great at organizing my own schedule, I was friendly when answering the phones, I could talk to people as long as I wasn't trying to sell them anything, and if I had the money, I could purchase a nice wardrobe. Right now, I had a few pieces that would help me get my foot in the door. Part of being an on-air personality was looking fashionable, and I was no stranger to aesthetics.

I'd hit rock bottom, and I knew it. I'd fallen fast without a safety net and only had a few weeks left before I was going to have to strike out for other parts of the country. If I couldn't find a way to afford a place to live, I was going to have to drive south. Maybe I could get a job in New Jersey or Pennsylvania, in a small town where the cost of living was drastically reduced.

It would mean giving up on my dreams and leaving the city that I loved, but it was looking more and more likely. The line began to move, and I got excited. A few more steps brought me that much closer to the door. Another two women went inside, leaving the rest of us still stranded on the doorstep.

I looked down the long line of prospective secretary's, hoping that I could outshine them. I guessed that a few had MBAs, maybe a few had worked for other CEOs. I didn't have either of those two boxes checked off, but I did have moxie and stamina. It was ridiculous. I was outgunned, and I knew it. I should just walk away and leave the job to the experts. But I stayed put against my better judgment. I had nowhere else to turn and no other rabbits up my sleeve. This job was the end of the line. Either I landed it, or I would have to turn around in defeat.

I wasn't sure why the employment specialist at the homeless shelter had turned me on to this gig. It wasn't the typical kind of job that opened up for those without means. I recognized the office as being one of the poshest in the city. Whoever worked there was bound to be rich and probably would never have experienced hardship. I didn't want to judge, but barring extraordinary circumstances, it was unlikely that anyone else working there was currently without a home.

I wasn't sure exactly what they did there. It wasn't a bank, and it wasn't a manufacturing plant. In a perfect world, I would have had time to do some Internet research. I didn't know what I was going to say in an interview if I couldn't talk about the specific industry I was applying for.

It looked like a money management firm, or maybe the corporate headquarters for a multinational conglomerate. Feeling ill prepared, I touched the shoulder of the woman in front of me.

"Excuse me," I said gently.

She turned around, giving me a smile that was at once friendly and a little bit nervous. She was obviously as worried as I was about landing the position. All of the other women in line were probably just as desperate as I was. At least some of them needed a win that day.

"Do you know what this company does?" I asked.

"It's in fashion," the woman answered.

I tried to remember what I knew about the fashion industry. I'd taken one economics class back in freshman year, and the focus had mostly been on countries and currency. "What kind of fashion?" I asked, feeling stupid.

"They have a few hot designers, but they also do down market sales. There's a lot of money involved," she replied, not giving me any trouble. If she thought I was out of my element, she didn't say so. "There are a lot of people here to apply."

"Yeah," I agreed. "I wasn't expecting so much competition."

"It's for a good position. Executive secretary to the CEO." She straightened up as if the mere mention of the title was enough to starch her spine.

"I know," I replied. The job counselor had told me as much. It was the only reason I was there, because that kind of title came with a paycheck that would allow me to live on my own.

Most people in Boston had a roommate or two, but I was on my own. I thought about answering some online ads for *roommate wanted*, but the thought of moving in with a stranger gave me the creeps. Beggars couldn't be choosers, so I really should just suck it up. The problem was at the moment, I didn't even have enough saved up to split the rent.

That's why I landed at the shelter, where I found a whole array of social services to help me. Some were more accessible than others. I could take a shower, but it was in a large room full of other women, and I didn't like that. I could hunt through the bargain bin for clothing, but it didn't fit well and was full of stains and holes. I could eat and sleep for free, which I did take them up on. The back seat of my car didn't provide the right support for my back, and I couldn't relax when I was out on my own.

Like a lot of people who found themselves homeless, I cobbled together what I needed and worked with what I had. Things were going to change, though; I could feel it. I didn't know why, but I was sure that this was my lucky day.

I'd chosen to wear my red hair down around my shoulders. Most of the other women were blond and had opted for ponytails or expertly coiffured buns. I knew how to braid my own hair and could have pulled it back, but I thought that the soft, ruddy curls gave me a friendly look. Whenever I went out to meet the public, I always wore my hair down.

I had a birthmark on my left shoulder that was much bigger than the tiny artistic spots that most women had to contend with. It covered my skin with a deep purple splotch, making it impossible for me to wear spaghetti straps or sleeveless gowns.

The collar of the shirt I wore neatly covered it up. And the high waistband of my skirt was at the height of professional fashions. If fortune was smiling on me, I would stand out from the crowd just enough to get my foot in the door.

It took me two hours of waiting in that awful line until I was finally in the building. The interviews were being conducted from two to five, and it was getting dangerously close to the five o'clock mark. I was terrified that they would round up the rest of us and send us all home without giving us a chance. But I was waved through at a quarter to five, allowed to get on the elevator, and directed to the tenth floor.

On the way up, I gave myself a pep talk. I was going to crush this interview. I was the person they were looking for; they just didn't know it yet. I had something that none of the rest of the bombshells had. I was organized and assertive, I knew what I wanted out of life, and I was hungry. That last adjective was the one I was going to lean on. Everybody wanted someone with hustle, whether it was in sales, in television, or in support services. I would prove myself by meeting every deadline and filing every report before I was asked. I just had to let the hiring manager know.

When the doors opened, I came face to face with the most gorgeous man I had ever seen. He had short, blond hair and shocking brown eyes. I almost stumbled, unprepared for such a vision. I recovered quickly, snapping my jaw shut. He looked tired. That would make my job that much harder. With no energy left to interview, would he even bother trying to act impressed by my meager offerings?

I screwed up my courage, determined to put my best foot forward. Stepping out of the elevator, I introduced myself. "Good afternoon," I said. "My name is Ava."

Chapter 3

Nate

I was considering punching my best friend. Peter Warren, better known as the VP of product design, told me without a doubt that a mass interview was the way to go. He had handled all the arrangements, putting the message out far and wide. The result was almost fifty different women all eager for the same spot.

Luckily, Peter had put a time limit on it. He said I would be available from two to five and promised me I would find someone by then. I wasn't feeling good about my choices. You would think that with so many applicants, at least some of them would be worth it, but that didn't seem to be the case this time around.

There were women who were beautiful and women who were competent, but I didn't feel any sort of a connection to any of them. I didn't want someone who was going to get into my pants, but she had to be in my head somewhat. I wanted a real partner, someone who would have my back in a meeting.

I wanted to be able to look at her and communicate things without speaking. If I needed her to rescue me from a particular client, or if I needed a break to sort things out, I wanted her to recognize those things. I just wasn't sure if any of the women I met so far were that tuned in.

Anybody could handle my schedule. Anybody could answer the phones. What I needed was a rockstar, and I hadn't found one yet. All that changed at the end of the day when the elevator doors opened and Ava stepped out.

I met her in the hall, just like I met all the other candidates. I had called down to the front desk to let them know that I intended to stick to the five o'clock deadline. If I didn't find anyone that day, I would return to the more respectable way of locating a secretary, through referrals. I would steal one if I had to.

I was still considering ways around the problem when Ava jolted me awake. She had long, red hair that swung free, pillowing over her shoulders and down her back. She was dressed appropriately, although not fashionably. The wardrobe wasn't an issue. We had plenty of lines of clothing we could use to outfit her. She wouldn't have to buy a thing.

It was her eyes that sealed the deal for me. There was a spark in them that went beyond the corporate environment. She was special, and she knew it. I felt some of my energy returning, and I found myself eager to sit down with her.

"Good afternoon," she said, presenting me with her hand. "My name is Ava."

"Ava," I repeated, noting just the right amount of pressure when I shook. "Nate Brockton. Call me Mr. Brockton."

"Pleasure to meet you," she said.

I turned away without answering, leading her down the hall toward my office.

"I'm surprised you're holding open interviews," Ava said, trying to maintain the conversational thread.

"It was the brainchild of my friend Peter," I replied. "He thought this would be the best way to find the right person."

"Lucky for me," she quipped, remaining standing while I circled my desk. "This is a lovely office."

"Are you from Boston?" I asked. I didn't feel the need to get right down to business. There was something intangible that I wanted to gauge, something about the chemistry between us that had to be right.

"Not originally, but I've lived here for a long time."

"Where are you from, originally?"

"Virginia," she replied. "But I was very young."

"Is your family here?"

She shifted nervously on her feet, and I could tell that I'd hit a sore spot. So the girl wasn't interested in talking about her family. Who could blame her? Family was a sore subject for me too, although everyone knew where I came from.

"Sorry," I said. "Family isn't relevant to the job. I just wanted to know."

"It's fine," she replied, shaking off the stress of my clumsy question.

"Tell me about yourself," I opened the negotiations, sitting down to signal the start of the interview.

"I have a bachelor's in journalism with a minor in theater." She settled into a chair opposite me, holding herself stiffly. "I had an internship with the local news where I was helping the journalists in the field."

"What kind of stuff were you doing?" I wasn't sure how a theater major was going to help my cause..

"A lot of getting coffee and fetching scripts but also I was sitting in on interviews and helping make arrangements."

"What kind of arrangements?"

"Like if we were going to interview someone at a bakery about their new scones, then I would call to arrange for the manager to sit down with our people and make sure to have a display of scones."

"Okay." That sounded like a skill set that could be useful. I would need someone to arrange for meetings and possibly travel. The logistics involved would be similar, although on a much larger scale. "Do you have experience keeping a schedule?"

"Yes."

"And making travel arrangements?"

"Yes."

"How's your typing?"

"Fifty-five words per minute," she replied.

That wasn't great, but it wasn't horrible. I didn't need a typist anyway; I just needed someone to help me stay organized and to greet people as they came into my office.

"What about computer programs?" I asked, already bored with the questions. Whoever I hired could learn Microsoft Office. It wasn't that hard, and there were plenty of online courses to teach it.

"I know Word, Excel, and PowerPoint," she said. "I'm good with Google, and I know some of the more popular project management packages."

"You know project management?" I sat up, interested.

"We used them in school," she replied, as if every woman I had interviewed with a degree should have been able to say the same thing.

"What school did you go to?" I asked.

"Lafayette."

I gave her a hard look, and she took it. She didn't squirm or look away. She didn't volley it back to me either. She simply held her head up and weathered my glance, the way a true aristocrat would. I was almost sold.

"Tell me honestly why you want to work here," I said.

This time, she did look away. I could see some of the determination leak from her shoulders and wondered what her story was. Everyone had their own reasons for wanting such a prestigious job. I was expecting a packaged answer about wanting to be on the cutting edge of fashion or wanting to grow within an international organization. But what Ava gave me was far more personal.

"I got involved with a man who wanted me to be someone I couldn't be. I tried to change myself to fit his idea of a perfect girlfriend. I moved in with him, and I thought that I was in love." She allowed her eyes to settle back on mine, her voice clear if a little bit soft. "I had plans to become a newscaster, but I got my priorities wrong. I thought he was more important than my dreams, and so I let myself get carried away."

I let her go, curious to see where it would lead. Her face was a study in light and shadow. Facing the window, I could see the sun dancing across her features. She held herself tall, even as she revealed her greatest weakness. I knew then that I had to have her—as my secretary, of course, not as my lover. She would be perfect to show people into my office, to maintain my files both digital and paper. She knew the meaning of hustle, and she needed the job more than anyone else. She was going to prove to me that she deserved every consideration I gave her, and I knew that motivation couldn't be bought.

"I want this job because I am fighting to win myself back," Ava said in conclusion. "I was diverted from my path, but I'm determined not to let anything stop me ever again. I will be the best executive secretary you've ever heard of, if you just give me a chance."

I looked her straight in the eye and said, "You're hired."

She blinked, caught off guard by my sudden declaration. "Really?"

"Yes, really. Let's get you down to HR." I picked up the phone and punched the button for HR. "I'm sending Ava…"

"Stan," she supplied.

"Stan?" I tried. It wasn't what I expected, sounding more like a frat boy than a leggy redhead.

She smiled, obviously having dealt with that particular brand of confusion before. "Yes, Stan."

"That sounds like a first name," I said.

"I get that all the time."

I checked with her again to see if she was joking, but her face held just the sort of long-suffering patience that one would expect from a person with an odd last name. I leaned on the intercom to continue my conversation with HR.

"I'm sending down Ava Stan. She's going to work with me. She'll need a badge and a computer and all that." I looked up at Ava, barely listening to the acknowledgement from the HR department.

"HR is on the second floor," I said. "Take the elevator down, take a left right out of the gate and it's the third office on your right."

"Left, right out of the gate, third office on my right," she repeated.

"Second floor," I said.

"Second floor," she parroted, getting it all straight in her head. "Thank you."

"You're welcome," I replied. "Don't let me down."

"No, sir."

I watched her walk casually from the room, not running and yet not dawdling. She had purpose to her step, something that I appreciated. She couldn't know how many cookie-cutter blondes I had interviewed in the past few hours, but she blew them all away.

Pleased with myself that I had solved the desk situation, and now the secretary problem, I belatedly realized it was probably time to do some actual work. I had a number of meetings I was putting off, but Ava could reschedule those as soon as she started. The best use of my time would be getting myself up to speed on the company. I was all in, and I knew as much as anyone, but there was always more to learn. For an hour I perused the quarterly reports then decided to pack it up for the night. I would get a fresh start in the morning—with a capable employee by my side.

Chapter 4

Ava

The whole way down to HR, I was shaking. I was so nervous that I was going to blow it, even though I already had the deal in hand. I kept myself stiff and polite, smiling often but not really showing any teeth. I made chit chat with the HR representative as she walked me through the steps to set myself up in the payroll system. She gave me a badge and a lanyard, checked my two forms of ID, and scanned my fingerprints.

"This is just to make sure you don't have a criminal history," she explained.

"Don't they do that at the police station?" I wondered.

"We just send the print to the police and they run the background check," the woman replied. "It's cheaper for us that way. Plus, it's a lot faster." She leaned forward conspiratorially. "It can take you up to a month to get a fingerprint appointment with the Boston PD."

"A month?" I repeated, acting shocked.

"With this, we'll get results by the end of the week."

"Does that mean I have to wait to hear from you?" I asked.

"Oh no," she said with a smile. "This is just a formality. You're scheduled to start tomorrow."

I held my breath. This was turning out even better than I'd hoped. Not only did I get the job, but there wasn't any waiting and wondering. I could start earning tomorrow, bringing me that much closer to my own apartment.

The problem was, when I finally got through the onboarding process and was let out onto the street, I didn't have anywhere to go. I wanted to celebrate. Taking myself out for a fancy dinner or some drinks would have been nice. But I couldn't afford to waste perfectly good money on fancy things.

I walked to the parking garage and got back in my car. It was going to cost me fifteen dollars to get the car out. HR had explained that I could buy a monthly parking pass from the garage, but that was way out of my budget. I needed to find a way around paying for parking. Maybe I could park outside of the city and take public transportation to work every day. That would solve the problem for a little while at least, until I was able to afford a spot.

I pulled up to the window and parted with some of my precious dollars. I wasn't assertive enough to ask for parking validation, and it hadn't been offered. I guessed sometimes people just didn't consider these little fees to be important. It was a big deal to those of us on a budget, but people who were comfortable in their jobs probably didn't even think about it.

I drove to the shelter, thinking that I could get a hot meal and take a shower. They let me in but told me that they didn't have any beds. That meant I was sleeping in my car. I took the news as gracefully as I could. It wasn't optimal. I couldn't really stretch out in the back seat, and the seat belt buckles poked into my back all night long.

But at least it was dry and provided some protection from the cold. And I had a job to look forward to. That fact alone could have kept me warm in a blizzard. I had a job, and I was on my way up.

I grabbed my toiletries bag from the back seat and a change of clothes. Locking the car door, I left it right behind the shelter, under the floodlight, in full view of the staff. No one would mess with my car when it was that visible. It was the dark alleys and corners that you had to worry about.

Swiftly, I walked into the locker room, avoiding everyone I could. There were a couple of old ladies standing naked in the middle of the room. I kept my eyes on the floor, hugging the walls. Past the toilets, there were four shower stalls. Two of them were empty, so I chose the one closest to the sinks.

While I had never been a victim of violence in the shelter, that didn't mean I let my guard down. There was no such thing as a luxurious shower. It was get in and get out, clean yourself up and move on.

I had to shave, so it was going to take me a bit more time, but I was a pro after so much time on the street. I could shave my entire body in less than ten minutes, add five for washing my hair and two for scrubbing my face, and that was all I needed. As I washed, I kept one ear peeled for trouble. It wouldn't do to get caught unaware while I was vulnerable. This wasn't prison, but it was the next best thing.

Without incident, I finished the shower, toweling off and slipping into what passed for pajamas on the streets. I couldn't get all comfy in jersey knit or a knee-length T-shirt, but I could wear sweatpants and a sweatshirt. That would keep me warm, and it was flexible fabric. If something happened in the middle of the night, I would be appropriately dressed to talk to the cops. But if I was allowed to sleep, I would be comfortable enough to get by.

I waited around until dinner was served. It was meatloaf, prepared and served by the congregation at Beth Shalom Synagogue. I always made sure to thank any volunteers who came into the shelter. They didn't have to spend their time and energy taking care of us. The home cooked meals were appreciated, and it didn't cost me anything to be friendly.

I got into a conversation with one of the women who was serving. She was going to MIT but preferred doing good works to partying and staying up all night.

"You're a rare bird," I told her with a grin.

She shrugged. "I've met so many great people doing this work."

"I haven't met that many great people," I responded. "Although hopefully I won't be here much longer."

"I hope you find your way soon," she said, turning back to the line and cutting another slice for the next homeless resident.

"I have a college degree," I told her.

She looked back at me in shock, her jaw dropping. Most people thought homelessness was a problem for the unemployed, for people who dropped out of high school or for military veterans who lost themselves in far-off battles. I didn't tell very many people that I was homeless, but if I did run into someone at the shelter, I liked to blow those preconceptions out of the water. If it could happen to me, it could happen to anyone. There wasn't any shame in it, although I wished desperately that my time out of doors would come to an end.

Leaving the shelter that night, I got back in my car and drove to a spot that I liked. It was in an alley behind a grocery store. There were lights all around, so I didn't feel so scared, but no one ever went back there after the store closed.

I parked the car and turned it off, climbing into the back seat. My phone was charged, so I used it to scroll through social media. Learning about how my friends were doing didn't make me feel any better about my own situation, but it didn't make me feel worse. Some of them had kids and pets that they showcased, making me smile. Some of them had lifestyles that they were promoting, like veganism or bike riding. A few of them were crazy, and their curse-filled rants made me feel like I was a pinnacle of mental health.

After browsing, I left without posting my own update. I didn't say very much online. The picture I used was from my sophomore year in college, and I hadn't bothered to update it. I knew that Marcus followed me, and I didn't want to clue him in on how I was doing. He could wonder, along with the rest of the world. I wasn't going to shed any light on the matter.

I set my alarm to wake up with plenty of time to get cleaned up and get dressed. The shelter opened at seven, and I had to be at work by eight-thirty. That left me an hour and a half door to door.

Drifting off, I wrapped myself in the glorious truth that this car camping thing was going away soon. I just had to get a few paychecks in the bank, and I would be all set. According to HR, I got paid every two weeks. So that was just one more month I would be living like this. After that, I could wake up in my own bed and take a shower without looking over my shoulder. I dreamed of that life and all the peace and security an apartment would bring.

It didn't feel much longer that I woke to the sound of my alarm blaring in my ear. Turning it off, I rubbed my eyes. I climbed over the seat and took the wheel, driving back to the shelter with plenty of time. I considered toweling off with some wipes like I had the day before, but thought better of it. I needed to make a good impression. A job interview was one thing when I wasn't sure about my chances. But the job was mine, and I needed it to stay that way. I would have to shower in the mornings, despite my distaste for the exercise.

I went through all the motions again and emerged from the shelter dressed professionally. I couldn't leave my car at the shelter all day, I was afraid for its safety and afraid that the staff would have it towed. I couldn't afford the parking garage, so I decided to park it somewhere close. Driving around the city streets, I was able to find a narrow lane without parking meters. Teasing it into a tight spot, I spent a good ten minutes fiddling until I got it right. Getting out, I locked the door. I had fifteen minutes to make it to work.

I hurried down the street, not altogether accustomed to the high heels I wore. Still, I was capable enough to make it on time. I showed the guard my badge at the door, and he told me where to swipe it. I punched through into the lobby, making a good impression on my first day.

With no wait, I rode up in the elevator to the seventh floor. Getting off, I found my way back to Mr. Brockton's office. I found the reception desk outside his office empty. I assumed that was where I would sit, so I tested out the chair, sliding a few of the drawers open to investigate. There were no files, pens, papers, or paperclips inside. It was as if the desk was new, or it had been cleaned out by a professional maid.

There was nothing on top of the desk either, so I had no way to do any work. There was a phone with several lines. I leaned over to read the text below some of the buttons. Forward, hold, line 1, line 2, that was all it said. It seemed pretty straightforward. I could handle that part of the job, no problem. I was going to have to ask about a computer, though, and there was no time like the present.

I got up and knocked on the office door. I waited a full minute before I heard a terse "Come in!"

Pushing it open, I walked through, familiar enough with the interior of the space to wait comfortably while my new boss finished up his phone call. He was on his cell, pacing the room. He looked at me, holding up a finger. I nodded to him. Of course I would wait.

I noticed a tray of pastries on a side table beneath a mirror. It was almost absurd, the dichotomy between Mr. Brockton's office and the shelter. There, everything was institutional, with dirty tile and peeling wallpaper. There were fluorescent lights everywhere and roaches scurrying in the corners.

But in the CEO's office, the windows were covered with fine drapes, a heavy netting that let in the light but blocked the glare. The carpet beneath my feet was plush and unbroken, either vacuumed fresh that morning or brand new. The space was wide and cool, broken into several different alcoves by glass walls and couches. The pastries were lying on a platter, next to a silver carafe that either held coffee or hot water. I tried not to focus on them, but I could feel my stomach rumbling. I hadn't eaten anything since the meatloaf last night. They looked delicious, all sparkling with sugar glaze.

Mr. Brockton hung up and glared at me, as if he wasn't expecting me or as if I had done something wrong. I shifted nervously in the spotlight, wondering if I made the right decision by taking the job. He seemed gruff and entitled, two things that were off-putting. But there was something that made me think there was more to him than a cocky exterior.

"You're right on time," he observed.

"Of course," I demurred.

"Are you getting settled in?"

"Yes, but who do I talk to about a computer?"

"Yes, of course." He crossed to his desk, checked something on his computer screen, and frowned. For a moment, I thought he had forgotten about me. He seemed so absorbed in whatever message he was reading. But then he resurfaced and gave me the information I needed. "Go down to IT. They'll take care of you."

"Where is it?" I asked.

"Fourth floor. Room 417."

I couldn't help tossing another longing glance at the pastries. This time, Mr. Brockton caught it and offered me one. I tried to stand on principle. I didn't want to look greedy on my first day. But he assured me that they were there for everyone, and he couldn't possibly eat them all himself. I would be doing him a favor if I took one or two off his hands.

I licked my lips, forcing myself to walk to the buffet instead of rushing at it. I picked up two jelly-filled doughnuts (because he'd said I could take two) and a napkin. Walking from the room, I couldn't resist biting into one. It might have been more professional to wait until I was back at my desk, but I was starving.

He gave me a quizzical look, which I just ignored. There was no false advertising involved. I was who I said I was. He didn't ask me where I was getting my meals, and I didn't offer it. If he assumed I was overly interested in breakfast foods, that wasn't the worst thing in the world.

I sat down to finish my meal before heading off to find a computer. It was a good thing that I took the time to eat, too, because I didn't have another chance. I had to spend hours getting through all the red tape before IT set me up with a desktop. And it was another three hours before I could sort through all of Mr. Brockton's appointments and make sure he was all set for Wednesday.

No one seemed to notice that I skipped lunch, and I didn't enlighten them. Not only did I not have the funds, but I didn't bring anything either. There would have been no point in taking a full hour off to sit in the break room and stare at my phone. I was ravenous by the time I got back to the shelter, and shepherd's pie had never tasted so good.

Chapter 5

Nate

It didn't escape me how Ava eyed the pastries. Personally, I didn't even like them very much. My mother ordered them on the assumption that I needed something to offer clients and visitors. They worked very well for that purpose, and occasionally I indulged. They were replenished every morning before I arrived, coming directly from the bakery down the street. That was another one of my mother's brainstorms. She thought it was important to support the local economy, and that by showcasing a local small business in that way, I could gain the approval of the city council or something. I didn't listen to half of what she said.

My father, on the other hand, liked to carry a big stick. He made a big deal about pushing startups out of the clothing market. If he saw a new designer who showed potential, he would scoop them up before they could pose a threat. It was his way of eliminating the competition. That, and sometimes he played dirty.

Years before, I saw him pick apart a rival company, trashing their brand until all they had left were boxes of product they couldn't unload. Then he swooped in and bought the whole thing for a discount, donating the clothing to some third world nation. It was all very petty.

I didn't know how my parents got involved with each other in the first place. They were polar opposites, as far as I could tell. Hopefully, I got some of the best from both. I liked to think that I could be savage when I had to be, and yet supportive and nurturing when life called for a softer hand.

I was getting those vibes from Ava. She was punctual and efficient, but there was something about her that was off. It had to do with the way she zeroed in on the pastries. I got the feeling that she didn't eat very much and that it wasn't by choice.

Most women I dated were averse to anything with carbohydrates. They wouldn't go near a pastry if their life depended on it. Ava was just the opposite. She took two every morning for breakfast, and I didn't see her eat anything for the rest of the day. Granted, I was busy and couldn't keep track of my secretary's break schedule, but I didn't think she was taking her lunch breaks.

I never once found her anywhere other than right outside my door. Her butt was planted firmly in her chair, and she answered every call on the first ring. I couldn't complain. In three days, she managed to clean up a year's worth of Lauren's crap. Suddenly I could find files on the shared drive, and there were notes for each of my meetings delivered to my inbox with plenty of time for me to read them.

I knew I'd made the right decision, but I found myself confused. What strange diet was she on that involved eating sugar for breakfast and absolutely nothing else? Why did she wait each morning for me to offer them to her, instead of just taking one? Didn't she recognize them for what they were? It was a shared plate of food, not my own personal pantry.

The next time I saw her, I decided to ask.

She came into the office on Thursday, ready to take notes. I was in the habit of rattling off things that I wanted to see happen, and I was pleased that she'd started bringing a notepad into our meetings. I opened my mouth to go over the day's events but saw her looking sideways again.

"You don't have to ask before you take one," I said.

She looked back at me with a wild and apologetic glance, as if she had just been caught with her hand in the cookie jar. I stood up, crossing to the opposite side of my desk so I could disperse some of the tension.

"Why are you so in love with the pastries?"

She looked away, an embarrassed smile on her lips. "I'm not in love with them."

"Are you taking your lunch breaks?"

She straightened to her full height, certain that she was in trouble. "No."

"You need to take your breaks," I said. "Your enthusiasm is appreciated, but there are labor laws."

"Okay," she agreed.

"Is there some reason that you're not eating except at breakfast?" I knew it wasn't any of my business, but I was curious. I decided to let her tell me that the topic was off limits, rather than just assuming that she didn't want to share. If I was wrong, I would let it drop. But if I was right, and there was a story behind her odd behavior, then maybe it was something we could work around.

She looked at the window, and then at the lamp. Anywhere but my face. When she spoke, her voice was clipped, her lips thin, and her eyes narrow. "I am currently homeless."

I didn't think I'd heard her right. "I'm sorry?"

"I am currently homeless," she said again. "I am sleeping in my car or at the shelter when they have space."

"Holy crap," I spit out before I could stop myself. That was the censored version. My original expletive was far less congenial.

"It's only until I get a few paychecks," she hurried on, distressed by my reaction.

"We have to find you a place to live," I said. I couldn't see any way around it. My company was my family's pride and joy, and the employees were important components of the machine. I needed everyone to be on top of their game, not trying to hustle for a bed at night. On top of that notion was a more personal desire to see Ava taken care of. I didn't want to admit that I cared so I let myself get angry. How dare she put herself in that situation? Didn't she realize that being my secretary came with responsibilities?

"I'm fine," she insisted. "It's really not so bad."

"Where did you sleep last night?"

"I don't want to tell you," she said.

"Tell me anyway," I commanded.

"In my car. Behind the Aldi."

I looked at her critically, searching for cracks in her demeanor. There were none. She was as stoic as a figurehead on a ship at sea, unfazed by the rough waters. I didn't like it one bit. I didn't want to think about her camped out all night behind some grocery store. I told myself that it was just for the company. We couldn't afford to have someone as talented and professional as Ava put herself in harm's way every night. There had to be some rule against that in the code of conduct.

"I'll give you an advance," I said.

"No, thank you," she replied.

"Well, you can stay in one of my apartments."

"I don't think that would be appropriate," she responded.

"What would be appropriate?" I challenged. "To let you sleep outside for one more night?"

"I'm doing fine, and I don't need help," she said, putting a little too much emphasis on it.

I could tell that she was wavering. She wanted her own place with a kitchen and a door that locked, but she wouldn't take it from me. Ava was stubborn, and she had her pride. She was embarrassed that I was going after her, forcing her to accept help.

My experience with most women was quite the opposite. I found that most of the females I entertained would be eager to accept any gift or trinket I might throw their way. Up to and including an apartment, I supposed. I really couldn't see any of my regular hook ups giving me a problem if I suggested elevating their standard of living.

With a heavy heart, I reigned in my protective impulses. I would have to be very careful in the future not to run over her with good intentions. I thought my money could buy anything. I had a yacht and real estate holdings up and down the coast, but none of that mattered to Ava. She wouldn't take a handout no matter how hard I pushed, and I respected that.

I wasn't willing to let the matter drop, though. She needed a home, and I wasn't going to sleep well in my own bed knowing she was out there somewhere sleeping in her car. It just wasn't right. I let it go. For now.

This time, when she attacked the pastries, she did so with some reluctance. She knew I was watching and that I understood what she was doing. I realized that they were probably the only meal she got, and that was why she needed two of them.

My thoughts went immediately to how to help her. She was too proud to take a handout, but maybe there was some way I could force her to see reason. She was one of my employees and therefore deserving of my assistance. That's what I told myself. I couldn't shake the disgust that visions of homeless shelters brought up and feeling helpless wasn't my strong suit.

Watching her ease her way out the door, her hands full of sweet treats, I decided to call my mother. Mariah Harris knew all about taking care of people over their objections. She was the queen of intrusive affection. If anyone would know how to help Ava, it was my mother.

Chapter 6

Ava

I almost expected Mr. Brockton to stop me from leaving that night. Throughout our conversation, he had that look about him, like he was going to assert his dominance. He was the leader of the company and my boss. I knew that if he wanted to put his foot down, he could. And then I would be left with an ugly decision. Would I stay on and accept his help, or would I quit and leave the only lifeline I had available to me?

If only I wasn't so hungry. Then I never would have devoured the breakfast treats, and he wouldn't be any the wiser. He would just go on believing that I was a regular employee with no problems to speak of.

It was actually kind of sweet, how protective he became. It would have been just as easy for me to accept his help, easier in fact than walking away. I thought about his offer of an apartment. Of course, he had several that were sitting empty, just waiting for tenants. I could put my paycheck toward rent, and in the meantime, I could live without worry. But that just wasn't who I was.

I couldn't accept a handout, no matter how forcefully it was thrust upon me. I needed to do this on my own. I didn't want him to think that I couldn't handle my own life. Just because I had taken a few wrong turns and ended up on the streets didn't mean I couldn't rescue myself. I just needed a little time.

In two months, I would be all set. Not much longer and I would move into a new place, and I would be able to afford food. I didn't need charity, but I did need the job. I hoped that he wouldn't force my hand. I felt like I was caught between a rock and a hard place. Yes, I needed the money, but I wanted to come by it honestly. To my relief, I didn't see him for the rest of the day. He didn't ask me to come back into his office and talk. And he didn't try to set me up with a place to spend the night.

I went back to the shelter and discovered they had a bed for me. At least I wouldn't be out there all alone. I ate dinner with the rest of the residents and went to my assigned cot to sleep. It wasn't the most comfortable bed, but it beat the backseat hands down.

Trying to get comfortable, I remembered sleeping with Marcus in his queen-sized bed, on a mattress he'd spent two thousand dollars on. It was firm and soft all at the same time. I'd never had a problem sleeping there, and while the shelter was better than the car, I couldn't relax completely surrounded by other homeless women. You never knew when someone would take an interest in you or your stuff. That meant I had to sleep with one eye open. It was a grim way to live, and I thought longingly of Mr. Brockton's suggestion.

Would it be so bad if I let him help me? If he gave me one of his apartments, then I could pay him back. I could work overtime. I could pay him back in installments. Anything would be better than this mean existence.

But I was too proud. I wouldn't let myself accept a handout. It just wasn't right. I went to sleep and dreamed of clean sheets. In the morning, I checked my belongings to make sure they were all still there. Luckily, no one had messed with them overnight.

I hit the showers again, getting in and out as quickly as possible. I avoided most of the other women if I could, although some of them were hard to miss. There was one little girl there with her mother, who refused to leave me alone. She followed me around the locker room, asking about my clothes and my toiletries.

"Do you have a job?" she asked.

I nodded, not wanting to get drawn into a conversation. I guessed she was about six, and I felt bad for her. It was hard enough being an adult in a place like that; I couldn't imagine what it was like for a child. She deserved a new apartment and a safe space to play more than I did. I wondered what the school thought about her living situation and realized that they probably didn't know. I wasn't alone in being proud. A lot of the women living in the shelter didn't advertise the fact.

Quietly, I slipped out of the bathroom when I was done with my hair. Wearing the same outfit I'd worn to the interview, I knew Mr. Brockton was going to judge. However, I didn't have that many professional ensembles. I didn't even have enough to wear something different each day.

That was going to have to be addressed. I couldn't let the rest of the staff know I was in dire straits. They would catch on pretty quickly if I rotated through the same three outfits every week. But I couldn't afford fancy threads. I had to save everything for the new apartment.

I took the car back to the same parking spot. I found that if I got to work early, there was almost always a place for me. This time all the slots were taken, and I had to drive a little farther away to find an open street. Parking, I glanced at the gas meter. It was trending dangerously toward empty, something that I would have to deal with before my first paycheck. It seemed like there was no end to the expenses I was incurring.

I climbed out and locked the car door. It was possible that I could borrow some money from the shelter for gas. They had a few programs designed to help working people. If they couldn't help me with gas, I was pretty sure that they had bus passes. Either way, appealing to the organization that was feeding me seemed like my best bet.

I arrived just on time, scanned my badge, and rode the elevator up. Before my morning meeting with Mr. Brockton, I sat down at my desk to get a few things done. Turning the computer on, I checked email to get a sense of what was in store that day. There were no emergencies and nothing pressing that had to get done. That meant I could work on the newsletter and the internal memos that Mr. Brockton wanted me to help facilitate. There was an entire graphics department and a publishing arm that handled communications, but the CEO was in charge of providing content. He asked me to gather some statistics from the quarterly reports and the names and stories of any new staff members, myself included. All of that was going to go into a friendly company email that would hit inboxes the following week.

I waited until it was nine-thirty, then grabbed my pen and paper and knocked on Mr. Brockton's door.

"Come in!" he called.

I pushed my way through, prepared for another morning prep session. Instead, I found he was already in a meeting. A beautiful woman with a shock of pink hair sat opposite the CEO, her legs crossed beneath a fashionably understated gown. I hesitated, not sure if I should interrupt.

Mr. Brockton waved me forward, and they both stood up. "Ava, this is my mom, Mariah Harris. Mom, this is Ava."

Mariah reached out a hand, and I shuffled my notebook around so I could reach for it. I was instantly drawn to her. Whether it was the comfortable aura or the warm smile, I couldn't be sure, but something about Mariah Brockton put me at ease.

"Ava," she said. "I've heard so much about you."

I shot a death stare at my boss, forgetting for a moment that he *was* my boss. He clearly had filled his mother in on my living situation. What else could she be talking about? I felt my spine stiffen. I didn't know where this conversation was going, but it couldn't be anywhere good. A mother was bound to have ideas about taking care of her son's employees. That must be why she was there, and what I thought was a meeting at first was looking a lot more like an ambush.

I shifted uncomfortably, not sure what to say. I didn't need to worry, though; Mariah went on as if there was no problem.

"We're so glad to have you on board," the woman gushed. "Nate has been telling me how punctual and organized you are."

I slid another scathing look at the CEO. Punctual and organized was the best he could come up with? I would show him. I was going to be the best damned secretary he had ever seen. That was if I could make it out of this room alive.

"Why don't you have one of the doughnuts?" Mariah asked.

"I'm fine," I lied.

"Nonsense." She walked over to the table that held the pastries and brought them to her son's desk. She then poured three cups of coffee and arranged them near the platter, so that we could all partake.

I sighed. It looked like she was going to feed me whether I wanted her to or not. She sat down in one chair, indicating that I should sit in the other. Mr. Brockton took his place behind the desk and reached for a cup. Like the devil himself, he took a pastry, biting into it with satisfaction. Mariah grabbed one along with a napkin to catch the crumbs. I had no choice but to follow suit.

The little breakfast treat was good. I was fast coming to rely on them to tide me over. They were a sweet, warm start to my day, and I had to admit that I was happy to be eating. It didn't escape my notice how Mariah orchestrated the whole thing. By joining me at the desk, she gave me permission to fuel my belly. It was almost as if she had experience encouraging reluctant people to take care of themselves.

"I get these from the corner bakery," she shared.

"They're very good," I said, glancing apologetically at my boss. It wasn't his fault that I was homeless. I shouldn't be so cruel when all he was trying to do was help.

He gave me a placid stare, one that would have been more at home in a poker game than a family breakfast. He was obviously very good at his job. I could only imagine that the ability to mask his feelings worked well in the boardroom. He was probably no stranger to tense negotiations.

"I think it's important to support our local economy," Mariah continued.

I could see she was working her way up to whatever she wanted to ask me. Well, I wasn't going to give her any help. We all knew that the real reason for this meeting was to discuss my situation. I didn't want to have that conversation then or at any point in the future. Maybe if I kept my mouth shut, they would let me off with just a friendly chat.

"Our company is international, but our headquarters are here in Boston," Mariah said. "We should be involved."

"That makes sense," I allowed.

"I made sure my husband—my ex-husband," she corrected herself, "supported the local little league teams."

"That's sweet."

"They have T-shirts with our logo on the back, and after each championship game, we give them lunch and trophies," Mr. Brockton said.

I licked sugar from my lips, listening carefully. They were trying to tell me that I wasn't the only one they were helping out. It was important to them to be a force for good in the neighborhood where they operated. They wanted to cash in on the health of the community, to generate a supportive environment for the company. I got it. When the change of subject came up, I was ready.

"I also work for a nonprofit that helps women get settled when they're leaving abusive relationships," Mariah said.

"I'm not in an abusive relationship," I replied quickly. "I'm not in any relationship."

"I know," she answered, just as quickly. "But my point is that we have deals with several rental units to help women establish residency and get back on their feet."

Tensing, I could see where this was going. I didn't want a handout. It was basically Mr. Brockton's offer of a free apartment restructured. Instead of accepting charity from the company, I would be routed through Mr. Brockton's mom's nonprofit. I didn't want to lean on anyone for help, but I couldn't figure out how to refuse.

"I'll be fine," I tried.

"Nonsense," Mariah scoffed. "The apartments are there to be used. At the moment, there are three or four available. What kind of employer would we be if we let you sleep in your car?"

"It's my business," I held my ground.

"Relax." Mariah softened her voice, reaching over to put a hand over mine. "We just care about you, that's all. This is no reflection on your abilities."

I opened my mouth to respond but shut it immediately. She saw right through my bravado and got to the heart of the matter. I wanted to rescue myself. It wasn't all about pride; I just knew I could do it, and I wanted a chance to prove myself. If I waited until that first or second paycheck and was able to get my own apartment, I would feel on top of the world. I would have a renewed sense of accomplishment at being able to turn my own fortune around. Mariah gently reminded me that no one in the room thought any less of me for being poor. They weren't judging. I was the only one with an agenda.

"Here's my card," she said, handing me a tiny rectangle of white paper. "If you contact me at that number, it will all go through the nonprofit. There will be no connection to your employer."

I accepted the card, feeling stunned. I looked over at Mr. Brockton to see what he thought, but he was busy examining some report on his desk. I was alone at the mercy of the sweetest bulldozer that ever lived.

"Thank you," I said, rising to my feet. "Is there anything else?"

"What does my schedule look like for the day?" Mr. Brockton asked, finally meeting my eyes.

"You have a video conference at ten-thirty, lunch with the VP of sales, and a two o'clock meeting with your Japanese distributor," I reported.

He nodded curtly, dismissing me. But before I could leave, Mariah stood up. "It's been lovely chatting with you, but I have to go."

"Thanks for stopping by," Mr. Brockton said, swinging his attention from me to his mother.

"Anytime, sweetheart," she replied. "Give me a call as soon as you can," she instructed me. "I'll let our secretary know to expect you."

I opened my mouth to object, but Mariah breezed from the room before I could gather my thoughts. Turning to Mr. Brockton, I let him have it. "You didn't have to sic your mom on me."

He raised his eyebrows, surprised by the vehemence in my voice. I couldn't help myself. All the feelings of inadequacy were coming up. I felt like he had staged an intervention, and I was the beleaguered alcoholic who couldn't get her life straight. I didn't need that kind of attention from him, and I certainly didn't need a free apartment.

After what Mariah had said, I was sure they would chase me down if I didn't call them first. They had a plethora of hiding places for battered women, and I would be doing them a favor by moving into one. All I would have to do was be grateful and I could move into my own place with no strings attached. It was too good to be true. I felt like I was losing control over my own life, and there was no one left to blame except Mr. Brockton.

"Stay out of my business," I warned him.

He watched me leave without saying another word. Arriving back at my desk, I instantly regretted turning on him. He was only trying to help. I wondered if he had ever felt lost for a single day of his life. Had he ever had to turn to anyone for help? Did he know what it was like to accept charity? Odds were that he didn't. He'd probably grown up in a mansion outside the city, going to private schools and coasting his way through college. He probably had a job waiting for him the moment he graduated and a fast track to the top once his dad retired.

So what if he was being kind? That didn't mean he could walk a mile in my shoes. And none of this helped my gas situation. I still had to eat, and I still needed the car to get to work. I put Mariah's business card in my wallet, thinking I would get to it later that day. It wasn't something I could avoid, but I could put it off for several hours. I had to think of a way to politely refuse her help. Either that, or I had to admit that I couldn't do everything by myself. And that was almost as painful as the reality of my situation.

Chapter 7

Nate

I was shocked and appalled by the way Ava treated me, but I put it down to obstinacy. She was more than capable of handling her own affairs, I was sure. I just needed her head in the game, and I wasn't sure I could get that if she was sleeping in her car.

I didn't want to admit that I was worried for her. Though I had only known her several days, already, I felt protective. I didn't want anything bad to happen to her, and the police statistics were rife with incidents of single women being attacked while walking alone at night. Her assurances that she was safe parked behind some grocery store were laughable. If I was a criminal and I found somebody alone in their car at night, I just might help myself to anything they had lying around. And that was the best-case scenario for that particular threat.

No, she had to have a place to live, preferably one with a kitchen and a locking door. And I wasn't above a bit of bullying to make that happen. Still, her acidic tone surprised me. I didn't expect her to turn on me for trying to help her out.

She was quiet and friendly for the rest of the day, but we both knew that I couldn't push her any further. I hoped that she would follow through and give my mother's charity a call. Mom hadn't been lying when she said there were several units that were empty at the moment. If Ava didn't want one of mine, she could damned well avail herself of a public unit.

I went home on Friday night without checking on her. Since she'd made it very clear that my attention wasn't desired, I would just have to trust her to connect up with the services she needed. Hopefully, she would see her way past her stubborn streak and accept my mother's help.

For some reason, I didn't feel like hooking up with anyone that night. There were a few women I could text, but none of them were exactly the person I wanted to be with. I got two invitations to go out for drinks, but I turned both down. I had a golf tournament the next day, and I told myself I needed my beauty sleep.

Fixing myself a brandy, I climbed into the hot tub on my deck. My first full week as head of the company was complete, and I felt good about the direction things were going. Ava was competent and smart, and with her by my side, I was prepared for every meeting I entered. After a lot of digging, I wasn't able to uncover any crises. It looked like Dad had left me with a pretty good ship.

They were working on the spring line in Paris, and the manufacturers for the down market stores were right on schedule. There was a bit of a problem with Italian imports due to a new law, but my legal team was on it, searching for a way around. Worst case scenario, we would have to scale back operations in that country for the time being.

I climbed out of the tub after about half an hour. Wrapping up in a bathrobe, I spent the rest of the night planted in front of the screen. I had a wicked video game system installed in my living room, with stereo sound and dedicated monitor. I logged on to the latest battle royale and gunned my way through multiple levels. It was a little bit of juvenile fun to let off steam, something that was becoming more difficult to carve out time for.

A while later, I went to bed feeling rested and woke up early to work out. I had a home gym on the first floor, complete with treadmill, elliptical, free weights, and a pull-up bar. There was also a smattering of more technology heavy offerings like a punching bag with sensors that measured the strength of my fists, and a bike with streaming classes. I hit the treadmill for ten minutes to warm up and spent most of my time on my back and chest. I had a routine that cycled through the major muscle groups, toning, not bulking. There was a very specific look I was going for, and that was fit, but not overpowered.

Thanks to my father, I overanalyzed everything about myself. He pointed out every word that I pronounced incorrectly, and every hair that was out of place. For a womanizing cliché, he was remarkably fastidious.

I had just enough time to take a shower and get dressed before leaving for the golf course. I was actually looking forward to the game. Peter was my best friend, and I had to admit his advice about the open interviews had been dead on. If I'd ignored him and gone the traditional route, I never would have met Ava.

"Hey, how's it going?" Peter said, holding out his hand for a slap.

I grabbed it and tugged, making a mockery of the traditional businessman's handshake. "Same old."

"Except you're president of the company now," Peter reminded me.

"And you're still a poor old VP," I teased.

"How's the new secretary working out?" He pivoted neatly to the next topic.

"She's working out well. I think it was a good hire."

"Not too bad on the eyes," he observed.

"I hadn't noticed," I said.

It wasn't exactly true. I was aware that Ava was attractive; I was just determined not to open myself to that kind of relationship. She was my employee, my secretary, for goodness' sake. I wasn't about to repeat my father's grave mistake and fall into the same category of offensive bosses who took advantage of their female coworkers. No, Ava was strictly off limits.

We connected with our caddies and walked out onto the green together. It was a small tournament, just among the patrons of the country club. That didn't mean it was devoid of fanfare. The club made as big a deal out of it as they could, with a breakfast buffet and a catered lunch afterwards. They had flyers printed and posted throughout the building, proclaiming the exclusivity of the tournament.

There was supposed to be a celebrity in attendance. She was a professional golfer, a high-ranking player in the LPGA. We all collected at the tee off, and there was quite a turnout. At least fifty people were in attendance, circled around the players. I spotted some family members and a few other club members I knew by name and reputation.

The prize for the tournament was ten thousand dollars. It wasn't a rich pot, but it was enough to qualify the event for the national golf publications. It was my third year competing, and I planned to donate the money if I won. There was a golf charity that held summer camps for underprivileged kids. It was generally expected that if anyone with means won the tournament, they would hand over their earnings to that charity. The only thing really on the line was bragging rights.

As I worked through the green, my phone kept buzzing. I looked down the first time to find that it was one of my regular hookups. She was asking about drinks and blatantly suggesting that we get together. I ignored it. I would answer when I had a minute to spare, but for the time being, I wasn't interested.

We were on the ninth hole when my father approached. I didn't see him at first, focused as I was on my swing. As soon as the ball left the tee and soared into the air, I heard his voice and cursed under my breath.

"Nate!" he called drunkenly.

I looked at Peter. "If I don't score under par, I'm going to blame it on him."

"I think he's spotted you," Peter replied dryly.

I turned around to greet my father, opening my arms for the obligatory hug. He dove right in, dragging me off my feet before slamming me back down again. Among my father's many annoying habits was his propensity to demonstrate his physical prowess. He had to be the biggest man in the room, and he never tired of proving his superiority. Or maybe he was just happy to see me; it was hard to tell.

I couldn't stop the wave of anger that crashed over me at the sight of him. What he did to my mother was bad enough, but the fact that he didn't even care about his secretary was almost too much. I thought if he was genuinely in love with another woman, that might have made a difference. His playing the field when he was married with a child felt like a betrayal not only to my mother, but also to me.

"Hi Dad," I said, putting on my game face. I was accustomed to hiding my displeasure. It served me well in business, as well as in golf, and it would also serve me well in my personal life, it seemed.

"How was your first week at the helm?" he asked, swaying a little in the sun.

"Are you drunk?" I asked. I couldn't help myself; it just slipped out.

"No," he snapped. "Just interested in how my son is doing."

"I'm doing fine," I replied testily. "It looks like you did manage to hand me a mostly functioning concern."

"What's this, *mostly* functioning?" he burped. "It's a powerhouse of a company."

"Congratulations," I said with a smile.

"I bet you fired Lauren," he accused me, pointing with an unsteady finger.

"Can we not talk about this now?" I asked.

There were other people around, some of whom were taking an interest. Peter looked away awkwardly, not wanting to get involved. I could tell he was anxious to go on to the next hole, and I couldn't blame him. I didn't want to drag the conversation on any longer than I had to.

"She was a good woman," Dad snapped.

"I don't care," I retorted.

"It's not her fault."

"She knew that you were married." I tried to keep my voice down, but the depth of emotion I was experiencing made that hard.

"It was over with your mother." My father wasn't giving me the same respect. His voice echoed across the green.

I turned away. There were so many things wrong with that statement. To begin with, it hadn't been over between him and my mother. They had still been married when he slept with Lauren. To add insult to injury, Lauren wasn't the only one that Dad had had extramarital relations with. I didn't know the names of the rest of them, but both Mom and I knew there were others.

It didn't matter. What was past was past. Mom was moving on, and I needed to as well. It just hurt, and to compound the injury, Dad didn't even appreciate what he had done. He thought it was meaningless, and that Mom and I were being overly sensitive. I wanted to throttle him, but the dozens of people who were looking but trying not to look like they were looking gave me pause.

I grabbed my nine iron and stalked off to the next hole. I kept my head down for the rest of the game, determined to ignore that ogre. I didn't know where he went after confronting me, and I didn't care. I wished I could revoke his club membership. That might prove to him that he had done something wrong.

I hated the cavalier way he aired our dirty laundry. Skeletons were supposed to stay in the closet, not be brought out to dance when there was company. Peter tried to make light of the situation, joking about how wild my father's hair was. I had to admit, he looked a little bit like Boris Johnson. The comparison was good, and it kept my mind from veering off the tracks into dark territory.

We didn't win the tournament. I wasn't surprised. After the ninth hole, my game was off considerably. The prize went to Steve Miller, an investment banker. I waited in line to congratulate him and applauded when he made the obligatory speech.

"I will be donating the prize pot to the Golf for Underprivileged Children campaign," Steve announced.

"Of course," Peter whispered.

"I would have done the same," I said.

It was a mark of success to donate the funds. Anyone who kept the money would be admitting that they needed it. The director of the charity came forward, acting surprised and happy, as if the entire event wasn't scripted.

I stayed for drinks at the club, avoiding my father at all costs. When I finally went home, I was spent. It was more the confrontation with my dad than the strain of the golf game. I was going to have to find a way to deal with him that didn't set off my fight or flight response. He was so aggravating, just the thought of having to talk to him got my heart racing. Luckily, I was in the prime of my life, and I worked out religiously. My heart could take it.

There was a message on my voicemail when I got home. For some reason, my mom still used my landline. I tried to disabuse her of that practice. No one even had a landline anymore. But it was a few dollars a month, and if it meant that I didn't miss a call, it was worth it. I don't know why she thought she could reach me at home. Even if I was there, I didn't pick up the phone.

"Hi, sweetie," my mom said. "I just wanted to let you know that we found Ava an apartment. We moved her in today, so she won't be on the streets tonight. Hope your tournament went well. Talk to you soon."

I pulled off my golf shirt, releasing myself from the stress of the day. At least one thing was working out. I wouldn't have to worry about Ava being mugged or worse. I walked through my home to the back where my gym was situated. Turning the boxing pad on, I settled in for a few punches. Each time I imagined it was my father's face I was punching. The output registered off the charts.

Chapter 8

Ava

I ended up calling Mariah's nonprofit because I didn't think I had a choice. If I was stubborn and refused help, she would hunt me down. She knew where I worked, after all. I was prepared to give some excuse as to why I didn't need an apartment. I could say that I was just waiting for my first or second paycheck, that I was really okay, but when I tried that line of reasoning, they shot me down.

It wasn't Mariah who answered the phone, but a case worker. She didn't want to talk about my situation over the phone and made me promise to come into her office for a consultation. I agreed reluctantly.

Still determined to get out of it, I showed up in their office on Saturday. I had an appointment at noon, and I arrived at twelve on the dot. I had almost no gas left in my car. It was starting to worry me. I'd applied for a small grant from the homeless shelter, but they wouldn't be able to process it until Monday. They had given me a bus ticket so that I could get around. But I didn't want to leave my car just anywhere. It had all of my things in it, and I had learned to be protective.

The charity was housed in a little brick building on the corner of one of the neighborhood streets downtown. They had a little lot in the back, and I coasted in. I grabbed my purse and went in for the consultation, fully intending to turn them down.

"Ava Stan?" the woman asked. She wore a short pink sweater and a pair of navy pants. I was dressed more fashionably than she was, but I knew that social workers often weren't paid what they deserved. She probably had kids at home and a mortgage and car payments, dozens of things she had to worry about before her outfits. Unlike the people I worked with, this friendly young woman probably shopped at thrift stores. There she could stretch her clothing budget, and fashion didn't have the same currency when you were working for nonprofits.

"Yes," I said, and stopped to sign my name in the guest book before following the woman to an office in the back. There were no decorations on the walls, and the entire space could have fit in a closet in my new office building.

"So how can we help you?" the social worker asked, taking a seat behind her desk.

There was just enough space in the room for two chairs, one on either side of the divide. I lowered myself into the visitor's seat and prepared to give my speech. "I don't really need help. I was just asked to come in by Mariah Brockton."

"Yes, she told me all about you," the woman agreed. I got the feeling she knew exactly why I was there, and that she would be as difficult to deter as Mr. Brockton's mother was.

"The thing is, I have a job," I tried. "I just need a few more weeks to get paid and then I'll be all set."

"We have short-term places that operate on a month-by-month basis," the woman replied. She was a no-nonsense kind of person who wasn't fazed at all by my admission of homelessness. "We could even do week by week."

I blinked. It hadn't occurred to me that this might be a temporary solution. Suddenly, the idea of being in a warm, safe space all by myself was almost as tempting as remaining stalwart. I tried to remember what I was doing there. I had come to turn them down, but in the space of a few short sentences, she'd almost won the argument.

"I'm staying at a shelter," I said.

"That's definitely an option," the social worker agreed. "But at the moment, we have several available spots, and it was important to Mariah that we get you settled in one of them."

I saw my avenues of opportunity closing fast. If I didn't come up with a good excuse soon, I was going to be out of options. "All I need is some gas for my car, and I'll be fine."

"We can give you a gas card," she replied graciously. "But you should really consider staying at one of our apartments. There's no commitment involved, and when your check comes in, you can start looking for a more permanent place."

I sighed. She was good. I would be crazy to deny myself the pleasure of a home, especially one that came with no strings attached. "I can't pay for it right now."

"The homes are free," the social worker said, her voice even and comforting. "We are grant funded through the state."

From my stay in the homeless shelter, I knew all about how grant funding worked. It was basically money from the government that was set aside to deal with social problems. It was how the employees got paid, and how the organizations paid for food, rent, and other things.

"Okay," I agreed finally.

"Great!" she said with a smile, opening a drawer to pull out a piece of paper. "Let's get some information, and then I'll show you to your new living space."

I had to give her two forms of ID. I used my driver's license and my work badge. We went through a bit of my personal history. Since they were a battered women's shelter, they asked me things about my previous relationship. I assured her that my ex wasn't interested in rekindling the romance, that he didn't care where I was and who I was with.

"It's just for formality," the woman assured me.

She asked details about Marcus's car so that they could place it on a watch list for their security guys. I had to explain how the relationship ended and the fact that he'd kicked me out. I told her that there were no children or pets involved, and that I had my own car and was gainfully employed.

After all that, she grabbed a gas card from a stack in her desk and a key from a locked box mounted to the wall behind her. I followed her out to the parking lot, where she got into her own car.

"Follow me," she said.

"Can we stop for gas first?" I asked.

"Sure," she agreed.

My little car made it to the closest gas station, sliding up to the pump on fumes. The social worker swiped the card, giving me just enough for a full tank. I felt the tension in my chest unwind and realized just how stressful it was to be low on fuel. It was a lifeblood to someone living out of their back seat. It provided a means for me to get around town, to get to work and to find shelter for the night. Having a full tank meant at least another two weeks of free travel, and I needed that.

After the gas station, I followed my new best friend around the corner. The apartment building was in a low rent area. There was no parking lot, and I would have to parallel park for the duration of my stay. That was fine. After so much time living on the streets, I was a whiz at that particular task.

When we had both parked, we met at the front door. The social worker held up one key, fitting it into the lock. Pushing the door open, we found ourselves in a narrow hallway. There was a staircase to the right, and we walked up one flight. Another hallway led away from the stairs, lined with apartment doors. The woman chose the second door on the left, holding up a different key. She unlocked the apartment and let me in.

It was the most beautiful thing I had ever seen. It opened up into the kitchen, which was really just a corner of a larger room. There was a refrigerator and a stove with a tiny chunk of counter space between. A sink lurked on the far wall beneath four beat-up looking cabinets. The floor was linoleum, a brown and yellow block pattern that was obviously decades old.

The living room consumed the rest of the space. There was a tattered couch and a mismatched coffee table. A television was set up against one wall, and a shelf beside it boasted dozens of DVDs. There were board games and novels as well, everything that I might need to entertain myself and others.

One door led to a bathroom and another to a bedroom on opposite sides of the living space. I peeked into the bathroom and found that it was dark and ugly, with brown tile and a single naked bulb screwed in above the sink. I didn't care. It was all mine for as long as I needed it.

The bedroom was furnished with a queen-sized bed and a single dresser with six drawers. There was a closet that held a few outdated dresses as well as some boxes on the floor. There were sheets and blankets folded neatly on top of the mattress, waiting for me to arrange them. It was everything that I needed to make myself at home, and nothing extra.

"This is a welcome basket." The social worker directed my attention to a brown box on the kitchen counter. "One of the local churches makes these. It has a few groceries and some snacks. There are also laundry tokens, some soap, shampoo, that kind of thing."

I looked at the social worker, trying not to cry. It was hard to accept help, but once I let myself, the kindness of strangers was overwhelming.

"There are emergency numbers on the door." She pointed to a laminated sheet of paper posted near the exit. "There will be a wellness check every Thursday."

I nodded, not trusting myself to speak.

"Good luck," the woman said, before handing me the keys.

I took them as if they were a lifeline. As soon as she left, I would be able to move my things in and lock the door. I could take a shower for the first time in a long time without having to look over my shoulder. And I could curl up on the couch watching one of their old movies, secure in the knowledge that I would be safe that night.

The social worker left me alone, and the first thing that I did was bring a bunch of stuff in from the car. I hung all my professional work clothes up in the closet, moving aside whatever was left from the previous tenant.

My belongings weren't plentiful; I had a few pairs of shoes, some books, and my sleeping bag. I also had two suitcases in the trunk that I hadn't opened since Marcus threw me out. They contained pajamas and pictures in frames, things that I needed my own place to display.

I knew I couldn't drive holes in the walls, so I leaned some of the pictures up on the windowsills. They were family photos, one of me and my parents, and one of a favorite pet who'd passed away several years ago.

Walking to the kitchen area, I investigated the welcome box and found some pretzels as well as a few canned food items. I would have to go grocery shopping soon, but this bounty would hold me over at least for the night. I also desperately needed to do laundry. That was another thing that would have to wait. My more immediate needs were relaxation, a long, hot shower, and a good night's rest.

The next day, there was a knock on my door that I wasn't expecting. I approached cautiously, pleased to see that it was my Mr. Brockton's mother standing in the hall. I opened up, expecting a burst of triumphant energy. I wasn't disappointed.

She gave me a hug without asking, bowling me over in the doorway. I stumbled back, holding tight to avoid falling. She didn't extend the greeting very long, pulling back as soon as she had made her point.

"What do you think?" she asked, surveying the apartment.

"It's wonderful," I gushed.

"It's crap," she said bluntly. "But it's just for a few weeks."

I closed the door behind us, turning to face her with a scolding look. "It took a lot to get me into this apartment. Let me just enjoy the vibes."

"Of course," she said with a smile. "Apologies. I just wanted to drop by and make sure you were settled."

"I'm getting settled," I replied. "There are some old DVDs I haven't even begun to look through."

"All donations," Mariah informed me. "The sofa, the table, the chairs, all tax write-offs for wealthy families."

"Please tell them thank you for me," I allowed.

"To be honest, you are exactly the kind of client that we hope for." She walked into the kitchen, opened up the refrigerator, and evaluated its contents.

"I think there might be some coffee," I said quickly, darting for one of the cabinets. I hadn't actually taken a look inside to see what kind of foodstuffs were available.

"Never mind," Mariah said. "We can go out for a cup."

"No really," I tried in vain to dissuade her. "I have to do laundry."

"You can do it when you get back," Mariah scoffed. "It will only take us a half hour."

I looked around the apartment, desperate for some excuse. I didn't want her to spend any more money on me. What she had already done was amazing. I had a place to stay and I had slept over ten hours, an unheard-of amount for either the shelter or the back seat. Normally five or six hours was ideal. On very rare occasions I got seven hours, but never any more than that. It just wasn't feasible when you were living in such close quarters with other people and things.

It didn't seem like I had a good reason to argue, though. And it was only coffee. I knew from previous experience that a few dollars for a drink wouldn't put anyone in the poor house. It was only the unemployed and the unhoused who couldn't afford the luxury.

I grabbed my purse and shoes and followed her out into the hall. Locking the door behind me, I felt a spark of delight. It was my place for the time being; I was the one who had the keys.

Mariah and I walked down the hall and out onto the street. A few blocks away, there was a local coffee shop. Like almost every establishment in Boston, it was small and cramped. There were about six tables in a narrow dining room, with seating that spilled out onto the sidewalk. Since it was Sunday, the place was packed. We ordered our drinks but had to sit outside. It was cold, but not painfully so.

I wrapped my hands around the paper cup, sipping happily. Mariah had insisted on buying some croissants. I ate without arguing. I still needed food, but I had no money to purchase it. I was going to have to make do with the canned food from the local church until I got paid. My choices were baked beans and chicken noodle soup, not the best menu. Still, beggars couldn't be choosers.

By the time our coffee was done, Mariah felt like an old friend. We walked back to my apartment, and she left me on the sidewalk. I gave her another hug impulsively before watching her walk away. It was good to be cared for. She was just an incredibly nurturing woman who was going through a hard time. What little she said about her divorce was illuminating. I hadn't thought about the problems other people were facing. Scrambling for my next meal had left me mired in my own heartache. I really felt for Mariah and appreciated all she had done for me.

On Monday, I was more than ready to go back to work. I felt like a million bucks, and it was all thanks to the little hole in the wall apartment. I showered alone once again, feeling like I could definitely get used to that. I wore my Monday ensemble, but this time it had been washed and ironed. I drove to work in a car that was devoid of personal belongings, and that fact alone made me feel free.

I still had to park far away and walk to the office since I didn't have the funds for the parking garage. But I was on time as always and slid in behind my desk triumphantly. When Mr. Brockton called me into his office, he was anxious to hear about how the new place was working out. I was so excited, I forgot to be angry, and just filled him in on all the amenities.

"There's an old Monopoly board," I said excitedly. "And there's a box of computer parts in the closet."

He tried to mask his amusement but couldn't quite accomplish the feat. I was sure that his place was a thousand times grander, but he had never slept in his car, so he couldn't appreciate the novelty of a roof and four walls.

Instead of pastries, he had bagels, and I helped myself to them without being asked. He joined me, and we sat eating breakfast together, talking about my windfall. It felt good to have someone to share my good fortune with. I hoped he would forget all about how bitchy I had been the previous week.

"So, what did you do over the weekend, Mr. Brockton?" I asked him.

"Why don't you call me Nate?" he replied.

I blushed, looking down at the carpet. I wasn't going to argue with him. It was a kind gesture, and on top of all the other kind gestures he presented me with, I wasn't sure how to repay him.

"I had a golf tournament," he continued, as if it was perfectly normal to ask his secretary to call him by his first name.

"How was that?"

"Fine."

"Did you win?" I asked.

"No," he sighed, looking away. "I was distracted."

"Do you think you could have won if you weren't distracted?"

"We'll never know," he said with a smile.

"How often do you play?" I licked cream cheese from my finger, happier than I had been in a long time.

"As often as I can." He watched me carefully, his lips curled into a gentle smile.

"Well," I said, finishing off the last bite of my bagel, "back to work."

I gathered up the trash and took it with me, depositing it in the trash can near my desk. It was amazing, but after two nights of restful sleep, I could devote all my energy to my work. I was astonished at the amount of energy I had to devote to my spreadsheets and emails. Everything I wrote sounded much more coherent. Every time I answered the phone, I nailed the conversation, getting all the right information from the caller to pass on to Nate. I had his schedule locked in for the day and the briefings on his desk well before they were due.

His statement about me being a better secretary if I got my living situation figured out came back to me. He had been right. I had been devoting at least half of my brain power to hustling for food and shelter. Now that I had at least one of those necessities figured out, I could be fully present at work. It was a good feeling.

I knew I was competent but having the energy to really apply myself was novel. I sped through my typing chores and opened all the mail. One of the VPs' secretaries asked me to help her organize a meeting. She was having trouble keeping track of all the RSVPs and there were two participants who never seemed to be available. I had extra time and energy, so I figured why not? I sent a few emails introducing myself and attached an online calendar poll to solicit information from the outliers.

By lunchtime, I had that extra project well in hand, turning it back over to the other woman. She was grateful, and I knew I had earned an important ally. In just two short weeks at this firm, I was fitting right in. Mariah had taken me under her wing, Nate was charmed, and the rest of the staff was appreciative.

Not only that, but I had finally landed on my feet. I had a place to stay until that first paycheck came through. When I had enough saved up, I could look for better digs, but until then, at least I had my own bed.

I took my lunch break, but I didn't eat. I wasn't entirely comfortable taking handouts, and I didn't want Nate to think he had to feed me breakfast, lunch, and dinner. He was clear about me taking my breaks, though, so I walked back to check on my car. It was right where I left it, all six windows intact.

Slowly, I walked back to the office, feeling revitalized by the fresh air. After lunch, Nate had a meeting with someone named Jonas Matthews. The man was all bluster. He breezed into the reception area as if he owned the place. I knew the type before he even said hello. He gave me that up and down look that said he would rather pay me for sex than for answering telephones.

I narrowed my eyes, trying to avoid as much of his attention as possible. I picked up the receiver to let Nate know that his two o'clock appointment was there. Jonas tried to make small talk with me as he waited. I remained polite but cold.

"You're an improvement over the last secretary," Jonas said.

"Thank you."

"Yeah, she was old."

I gave him a tight smile.

"What do you think of Mr. Brockton as a boss?" Jonas leaned against my desk.

"I think he's waiting for you," I replied, looking up into his eyes as tactfully as I could.

The man glanced up to find the door open. Nate stood in the doorway, glancing our way. He pushed the door open even farther, ushering Jonas in. I rolled my eyes, and Nate caught it. I saw him suppress a smile before disappearing into his office behind the offensive guest.

It was my first experience with such an asshole. I hoped it would be my last. Despite the fact that everyone in the building was swimming in wealth, they were all by and large decent people. No one else made me feel like a piece of meat, and I appreciated that.

I forced myself to concentrate on my work, not worry about the end of Nate's meeting. I couldn't help going back to study the notes I had collected on Jonas Matthews. He was an entrepreneur who was trying to get into the fashion industry. He'd made some waves with good investments early on, so he wasn't someone to ignore. I didn't know what he wanted with Nate, though. If Jonas bought into another clothing company, he would be in direct competition with Nate. That alone should have scared him off, but he insisted on sitting down with the new CEO, and Nate reluctantly advised me to make space in his schedule. I hoped this would be the last such meeting. I had only just met Jonas, and already I didn't like him.

I was so efficient that I had a few extra minutes with nothing to do. I had to stay by the phone in case it rang, but I didn't have anything else in particular to work on. I opened social media on my phone and began to scroll, stalking a few of my old friends.

When Marcus and I were heavily involved, he'd encouraged me to drop all my other relationships. That meant ghosting women I'd gone to college with, people I had known since high school and everyone else in my life. It was nice to check up on them, to see where they were and how they were doing.

I put my phone down when I heard the doorknob turn. Both Jonas and Nate emerged at the same time. Jonas was talking and Nate was listening, but it was clear to me that Nate was just being polite. He wanted the other man out of his office, and he was taking matters into his own hands.

Jonas paused on the threshold, spotting me in the same place he left me. "You gotta watch out for this one." Jonas pointed a finger at Nate.

I exhaled softly, forcing myself to remain calm. He was pushing all my buttons without even realizing it. I didn't know if he could be more chauvinistic if he tried. It was like someone had collected all the outdated macho crap in the city and poured it into human skin.

"I hope I'll be seeing you soon," Jonas said on his way out, winking.

I turned to look at Nate and found him glaring openly. It was a relief to know that we were on the same page. I didn't have to worry about him inviting Jonas back any time soon. I wanted to ask what that had been all about, but it was none of my business. Nate spared me an exasperated look before disappearing back into his office. I left my phone where it was on the desk beside me and went back through my emails to make sure I hadn't missed anything. There were still two hours left in the day, but I knew I couldn't play on my phone any longer.

Chapter 9

Nate

Jonas was annoying. There was no better way to put it. He had a lot of ideas, but he didn't know when to take a back seat. He wanted to pitch a million things at me, and when I came up with reasons I couldn't run with each of them, he didn't slow down. He just pivoted and moved on to the next in an endless stream of ideas until I finally stopped him.

"What is it you want from me?" I asked.

"Your time," he answered. "I think I've got a great concept, and I'm interested in going into the athletic fashion industry. I just need a little mentoring."

"Mentoring?" I couldn't believe it. It was worse than I thought. He didn't want me to acquire any of these ideas he was promoting; he wanted me to help him see them to fruition. That could potentially take more time than just doing them myself.

Not that they were all bad ideas, but I was busy enough running my own ship. I didn't have time to sit down with Jonas every week or every other week or even every month. But I had a sneaking suspicion that denying him would have consequences.

He had all the right connections. He went through the club, through a mutual friend who I also didn't want to disappoint. Jonas went to the right schools, and he tossed names out left and right, letting me know that he was a rising star. His implication was clear. If I refused what he was looking for, he would take his considerable moxie to the next billionaire. I would earn myself a sworn enemy, and potentially lose customers.

The threat of startups was real. In the tech space they were legendary, but even in fashion, you had to be careful. "Hip" was an adjective applied easiest to young upstart companies, not old established ones. I could invest heavily in designers to stay current and trendy, but at the end of the day, my brand was already known. I couldn't make the jump from affordable, practical clothing to cutting edge athletic gear overnight. He could.

He had the money and the connections to hire designers and begin manufacturing. I could either play mentor and earn a friend, or I could kick him out and gain an enemy. I didn't actually want to do either. What I wanted was to be left alone. But I didn't have that option.

I finally said I would think about it. I made up some excuse about having to clear enough space on my schedule, and I asked him to get in touch with Ava. Then I walked him to the door, not giving him time to get into Ava's business.

He seemed to forget all about making an appointment when he saw my secretary again. I didn't like the way he looked at her. It was as if he was imagining her in some compromised position. I saw she noticed it too, and the icy stare she gave him would have turned off most men. Jonas Matthews was not most men, however. He had to be encouraged to leave. I walked him to the elevator, making sure to push the button that would take him back to the lobby.

I returned to Ava's desk. "What a jerk."

"Where did you find him?" she asked.

"Friend of a friend," I responded.

"He's…enthusiastic."

I laughed. "He is that. Have you taken your break?"

"I did," she said.

"But did you eat?" I asked the follow up question, knowing implicitly that the answer was no.

Ava shook her head, favoring me with a shy smile.

"Come on," I went back into my office to grab my wallet, returning a moment later. "Let's go get a slice of pizza."

"I can't let you take care of me all the time," she argued. I was pleased to see that even though her words were dismissive, her body language wasn't. She stood up, prepared to follow me to the door.

"It'll be a working lunch," I told her. "I need to decompress after that meeting."

"I'm not surprised." She joined me in the elevator. "The man is like a verbal octopus."

I turned to face her, considering that metaphor. "He is," I agreed. "He had a lot of ideas, and I couldn't get a word in edgewise."

"What did he want?"

"Essentially, he wanted to threaten me."

Ava gasped, her pretty eyes flashing wide with shock. "Oh my gosh."

"It's not as dramatic as all that," I assured her. "He wants to start his own clothing line, and I can either help him by mentoring him, or he'll forge ahead without me."

Ava relaxed, her visions of me being held at gunpoint or whatever it was that had captivated her, replaced by a more realistic picture. "That doesn't sound so bad."

"He has the money and the time. He could be a serious competitor," I replied, annoyed with myself for being so hung up on the prospect. I had dealt with startups before. I could just wait until he reached a certain market share and then buy him out. I didn't need to validate him with my attention.

When the elevator stopped, I held the door open for Ava. She walked through, giving me time to get ahead of her again. We left the office together, completely ignoring the security guard. He was well paid and wouldn't spread any gossip. Besides, I was free to have lunch with whomever I wanted to. It didn't mean anything.

There was a pizza place within walking distance. I turned right and started down the sidewalk. Ava came alongside me and we talked about the schedule for the rest of the day and the next. Since what we had in common was mostly office related, it was easy to stick to work topics. I didn't feel uncomfortable with her though, or like I was standing on ceremony. In fact, her presence was almost friendly.

We ordered at the counter and grabbed our drinks and sat down. I chose a spot near the window, so we could see people walking by on the street. It was cozy, but somehow also boisterous. There was a baseball game on television and the few screens scattered around the place were all synchronized to the same channel.

Ava made some comment about one of the players, making me realize that she was following the season. It was a nice surprise. For some reason, I didn't expect her to be that into sports and being proven wrong was an unexpected bonus. I was pretty good at reading people and for someone to exceed my expectations was rare.

My phone beeped while we were talking and I checked it. It was Jill, one of my regular hook ups. I decided to stop putting her off and give her a call later that night. I answered the text to let her know that I was busy, but not ignoring her. She approved with a thumbs up emoji and we left it at that.

Something about being around Ava made me feel a little more amorous than usual. Since Ava was obviously off limits, I would have to find companionship elsewhere. Jill was fun and low maintenance. We had a very casual relationship, bordering on no relationship at all. She just occasionally texted and I occasionally texted her back. We met up when we did and didn't sweat about it if we failed to connect.

I wished everything in life was that easy. For one traitorous moment, my mind went to how nice it would be to have a similar relationship with Ava. I could take her home with me when I wanted to, and we could have fun together without consequences. We wouldn't have to mar the office with a sordid affair, but we could let ourselves explore something more than just a professional friendship.

I put a stop to that train of thought as soon as it pulled into the station. There was no way I could occasionally sleep with my secretary and have it not affect the business. If I learned anything from my dad, it was not to date the people I worked with. I needed Ava to be sharp and focused on her job. I needed to keep the workplace drama free for my own sanity as well as the bottom line.

No, Jill was the way to go. I could take her out for drinks and escort her to my place for a night cap. She would leave in the morning and we would each resume our own lives. It was perfect. I just wasn't sure why I felt so guilty about texting another woman while I was at lunch with Ava. It's not like we were on a date. This was just work. Wasn't it?

Chapter 10

Ava

After just two weeks, I was beginning to get my sea legs. I knew where all the rooms were in the building and I had made a few friends. I recognized other secretaries and salespeople by name and was building a reputation as someone who got things done. Everyone was super kind and helpful whenever I was lost. It seemed like one big family, and I was working for the boss.

Mr. Brockman, or Nate as he asked me to call him, was the best employer I ever had, hands down. He was never cross with me, and always appreciative. He went out of his way to thank me every night before I left. I would poke into his office and ask if there was anything I could get for him before I left. He would either ask for a document or tell me he was fine. And before I walked out the door, he would say "thanks."

I learned that he came into the office early in the morning and worked late at night. He didn't seem stressed though, just busy. He always had time to go to lunch and to stop and have breakfast when I came in. I began to look forward to our bagels or croissants with coffee, eaten at his desk.

He shared his lunch with me as well, ignoring my complaints. Whenever he ordered delivery, he ordered two of everything so that I could have one. If he had a lunch meeting, he would make sure I was in on the lunch order. I stopped arguing after the first week. I made a pact with myself that I would pay him back every single penny once I got my first check. It was silly. The man was a billionaire, he could afford $7 a day to feed his secretary. But I didn't see it that way. It was a matter of pride, and I didn't want to be a freeloader.

That first check was a godsend. I found it on my desk the second Friday. I supposed that HR must have dropped it there before the building opened. I knew what it was the moment I saw it. Nothing else looks exactly like a paycheck.

I tore into it, careful not to rip the check itself. Stunned by the number, I sat down heavily. I knew the salary was impressive, but somehow, it still surprised me. I would have enough from just one paycheck to pay rent on the place I was living at the moment. It was also enough to trade up to another apartment, although not enough to pay first and last month's rent plus a security deposit. I would still need at least one more check before I could move out on my own.

But with the efficiency apartment mine for the time being, I wasn't worried. Mariah and the social worker said I could stay for up to six months if I needed to. And I could stay month by month, so that as soon as I was ready to move on, there would be nothing holding me back.

I considered spending some of the money on clothes. I was in desperate need of a wardrobe upgrade. It was becoming embarrassing only having three outfits to cycle through. People were unfailingly polite, but I could tell that some of them were beginning to notice.

I would have to swing by the bank. I wasn't sure why I got a paper check. I thought that I gave HR all my information for direct deposit. Sending an email, I just had to be sure that all my forms were in. They answered an hour later, telling me that the first and last paychecks were always paper copies. Afterwards, I wouldn't have to bother with the formality, and the money would be dumped straight into my account.

Throughout the day I kept sneaking peeks at it. It was beautiful, and not only that, but it meant a lot of really good things for me. I could pay Nate back for all the lunches that he bought, and I wouldn't have to accept charity from him again. I might even be able to buy a cup of coffee for myself before work. That thought alone sent me into a dream state, imagining a steaming cup of fancy coffee with whipped cream and mocha or whatever it was that the glitterati drank.

I could put gas in my car and go grocery shopping. I might even splurge and buy some snack foods. I was so accustomed to eating only what I could scrounge from the office, from the shelter, and from the canned goods left behind by church goers, that I completely missed chips and popcorn. They just weren't accessible.

Another thought hit me as soon as I opened the door to snack foods. I could buy ice cream. I could sit in my own living room, eating ice cream from a pint with a spoon, watching one of the old DVDs the charity left for me. The thought was almost orgasmic, and I made a date with myself to do just that as soon as the check cleared the bank.

I was ready to buy my own lunch but realized that I needed to deposit the check first before I could spend it. That meant one last meal courtesy of Nate. Or not. I didn't want to ask him, and I was feeling so good about my impending party of one that I didn't even need fuel.

My phone beeped, drawing my attention back to the real world. Checking the screen, my heart fell even further. It was from Marcus. He was angry that I was going out with another man. I was taken aback. I didn't think he cared. It had been more than a month since he kicked me out, and I hadn't heard a word from him.

He was the one who ended it. What gave him the right to comment on my love life? And when had I ever been out with another man? I tried to reconstruct my steps from the past few days, but the only possibility I could come up with was Nate. We shared lunch a few times, but it was nothing serious. Marcus couldn't possibly be talking about my boss, could he?

That would mean that he was following me. That was a terrifying thought. How else would he have learned about my lunch dates? Maybe he was just innocently in the area, and had seen me disappear into the pizza place with Nate by my side. But innocent wasn't exactly the word I would use to describe Marcus. He was more like a tyrant.

I promised Mariah and her domestic violence shelter that Marcus wasn't dangerous. Suddenly, I was thankful that they made me describe his car. That meant that someone was looking out for me. They had experience with abusive partners who tried to reach out to women living in their apartments. I thought I was different, but maybe I was wrong.

The text scared me and made me wish that he didn't have my number. I blocked him from texting me again and considered changing my number. I didn't have that many friends who contacted me that way. It might be worth looking into. I could always update my file with HR, and let Mariah know what I was doing.

For the rest of the day, I couldn't shake the icky feeling that Marcus was following me. There was so much vitriol loaded into his words, I lost all enthusiasm for my ice cream party. When I looked at my check again, it gave me a shot of adrenaline. It was still every bit as spectacular as it had been that morning, and nothing about it had changed. I was going to be able to pay my own way pretty soon. Marcus would forget about me, and I would forget about him, and we would both move on with our lives.

I struggled at first, but I was on my way back to the top. I couldn't let my ex get under my skin like that. I was safe at work, and I was safe at home. Whatever Marcus wanted to think or get worked up over was his business. I didn't have the time or emotional energy to worry about his drama.

At around three o'clock that afternoon, Mariah came into the office. She brought with her two assistants who each had three garment bags with them. Nate was in a meeting, so I greeted his mother myself.

"He'll just be another half hour," I told her.

"It's you I came to see," Mariah dismissed my concerns.

"Really?"

"Well, you and him," she amended her statement. "We have some clothes we want you to try on."

I looked at the two assistants, uncertain whether to believe Mariah or not. "I'm not a model," I hesitated.

"These are just samples from the first run," Mariah explained. "We don't need a model; we need an ordinary woman to wear them for a few days."

"Oh," I swallowed all the rest of my objections. "What happens after a few days?"

"You can keep them," Mariah replied triumphantly.

One of the assistants draped her collection of garment bags over my desk. She pulled out one bag and unzipped it, allowing me to see the contents. I stepped close, delicately sliding the black plastic out of the way. Inside was a gorgeous pink and yellow dress with flowy sleeves and a layered skirt. Beneath that was a blue and white power suit with a trim belt and broad lapels.

"How many of them are there?" I asked, stunned.

"Two or three per bag," Mariah said.

I looked up to find her watching me with a look I could only call maternal. I gave her a hug. I couldn't help myself. It was all too much. I wasn't sure if they actually needed someone to try on the clothes and wear them around, but I didn't care. It was just feasible enough for me to swallow.

"How am I going to get these home?" I asked.

"We'll take them to your car," Mariah announced, checking with her assistants.

"Yes ma'am," one said.

"I'll show you where my car is." I grabbed my keys from my desk drawer.

"Later," Mariah scoffed.

The assistants looked uncomfortable. The bags were probably heavy, and they were forced to act as glorified porters. "It'll just take a minute," I lied, to get them off the hook.

"Okay," Mariah relented. "But hurry back. And leave one of the bags here, I want to see how they look on you."

I shuffled the bags around to leave the first one on my desk, picking up the other two and walking toward the elevator. Both assistants followed me, the first one accepting the burden back despite my protestations.

I showed them to my car, which was parked a good distance away. They didn't ask why, and I didn't offer. I knew they were expecting me to be parked in the garage, and that the extra few blocks were a hassle they hadn't counted on. But I didn't have the money to make their lives easier, and I didn't have the balls to tell them that. So, I just kept my mouth shut and let them wonder.

Back at the office, I tried on the yellow dress first. Mariah asked me to spin around, and I felt a little bit silly. It was fun to try on new clothes, and to feel like a fashion icon. A little bit of my birthmark was visible below the dress. The neckline wasn't what I would have chosen for myself.

Mariah either didn't notice or was too polite to point it out. The assistants didn't seem to care either. They promptly sat down on the couch in the waiting area and pulled out their phones.

When Nate came out of his meeting, Mariah went to him, eager to show me off.

"What do you think?" Nate's mom asked, taking her son by the hand.

"Impressive," Nate approved.

I don't know why his opinion mattered so much, but it did. I was pleased that he thought I was pretty. Sewing my old outfit up in the garment bag, I hung it on the coat rack in Nate's office. I wore the yellow dress for the rest of the day, not caring what anyone thought.

Chapter 11

Nate

I straightened my cuffs, glancing at myself in the mirror. After a morning workout, followed by a shower and a shave, I was ready to go out. Friday night had been fun but the traditional rules of when to work and when to take off didn't really apply to CEOs. I had a lunch meeting with a financial backer, someone I had to impress with my willingness to work on Saturday.

I buttoned my shirt all the way up, ignoring the stiff feel of the cotton against my throat. There would be plenty of time to unwind after the day's meeting. It was only lunch. I slid my arms into a suit jacket and knotted my tie. It was game time.

My phone buzzed when I was halfway out the door. I rolled my eyes. It was my mother, demanding attention. I stopped to text her, letting her know my plans. She insisted I stop by after lunch and spend some time with her at her new penthouse. I couldn't think of a way out of it, and I didn't actually have anything planned for the remainder of the day, so I agreed.

The lunch went off well. I was able to rattle off some first quarter numbers that sounded good. I didn't have all the reports memorized, but I promised that Ava would send them over first thing Monday morning. It was more about showing up and promising to do a good job. Under my dad's leadership, the banks always got their cut. It was up to me to continue that tradition and they just wanted to make sure I knew it.

I knew quite a lot about operations, enough to keep the conversation going. I didn't try to impress him. He knew all about our company and how much of a fixture we were in the industry. All I had to do was let him know that the business was in good hands.

We parted around one, having both accomplished our objectives. I drove over to my mother's place, parked, and walked up the drive. She lived on the top floor of a quaint little building that had been recently restored. The front door was open, which I didn't like. I would have to speak to her about getting a buzzer put in.

It was my first time visiting her place and I was evaluating everything with a critical eye. It was definitely in a safe neighborhood, and to my knowledge Mom didn't have any enemies. But I would still feel better if the front door was locked and the residents were the only ones with keys.

I went up to the third floor and found myself on a small landing. There was nothing but a door and a small patch of floor to stand on. I knocked and heard the sounds of movement within the apartment. A moment later, my mother opened the door, standing back to allow me entrance.

She wore one of her many flowing robes, this one with wizard sleeves and a muddy brown tie dye swirl. For the ex-wife and mother of fashion executives, she could be a little tone deaf on the current trends. I appreciated the nostalgia of the 1970s, but it wasn't exactly in keeping with the times.

I kept my criticism to myself. It wouldn't help our relationship and she didn't care what I thought of her dress. It was the apartment I was there to see. She wanted to show it off and she made no secret of it.

"What do you think?" She wandered into the living room, waving her hands in the air as if she could conjure up the spirit of the place.

"It's nice," I approved. High ceilings, plenty of natural light, hardwood floors, the place had it all. It was big too. No closet living for my mother. There was a generous living room that swept toward a galley sized kitchen. To one side was the hallway that led to two bedrooms, one for my mom and one for guests. There were two bathrooms, one off the primary bedroom and one on the opposite side of the living room.

She had a television, but I knew she didn't use it. It was probably just a prop left over from when the real estate agents staged the place. My mother's favorite artwork adorned the walls: colorful oil paintings in abstract colors and geometric shapes.

"It's perfect for you," I amended my first response.

"Thank you." She gave me a kiss on the cheek. "What was this meeting all about?"

"One of Dad's old banker friends wanted to make sure I'm not a damned idiot," I told her.

"And did you show him you're not?"

"Of course." I followed her into the kitchen where she poured me a glass of juice. I wasn't actually thirsty, but I accepted it anyway.

"Not a difficult task," she observed.

"No," I agreed.

"What did you think of the new line on Ava?" Mom winked and I could tell she was insinuating something.

"It's a great line. It should fly off the stores when it debuts." I took my drink back to the living room and sat down.

Mom followed me, her bare feet padding across the floor. "That's not what I meant."

"I have no idea what you meant then." I gave her a sharp look, trying to discourage her from taking the insinuation any further.

"She's a wonderful girl," Mom continued, oblivious to my warning.

"No." I shut her down.

"What?" She acted innocent.

"No, I'm not interested in Ava that way."

"I didn't say you were."

"She's a wonderful girl?" I parroted Mom's previous statement, twisting it just enough to make it seem sinister.

"She is!" Mariah gasped, as if I had offended her.

"I have no doubt." I felt my voice rising and fought to control it. "I just don't like her like that."

"Nor should you," Mom relented, giving up the chase.

"Okay." I put my hands up in mock surrender.

"Admit it, you're happy she's off the streets," Mom came back at it from a different angle.

"I am thrilled that she's off the streets," I replied. "But not because I want to date her."

"Oh, honey." Mom wrinkled up her nose, "Let's not be crass."

I shook my head. I couldn't win. Apparently, she was free to make all kinds of improper suggestions, but when I called her on it, I was the dirty one. I knew the only way I was going to get out of the conversation was to turn it around to other things. The divorce was a touchy subject and Mom wasn't really involved in the day-to-day running of the business. She didn't play golf and she didn't play video games.

"Have you heard from Aunt Polly?" I asked. My mom's sister was a train wreck and always a good topic of conversation.

"Oh, you'll never guess what she's up to now," Mom took the bait, launching into a discussion about Polly's latest scandal. She was dragged into some kind of pyramid scheme that involved selling organic household cleaners. The problem was that Polly had already sold bottles to everyone in her immediate circle, including my mom. "It's good, and it smells nice, but it doesn't work any better than the cheap stuff. And I'm not going to keep buying spray cleaner from my sister. She has to ship it from California. It's crazy. I would do much better just going to Whole Foods."

"So what is she going to do with a closet full of cleaning supplies?" I asked.

"Open her own maid service?" Mom guessed, laughing at the absurdity of the idea.

"Maybe that's where she should sell it."

"But she's not making any profit," Mom reminded me. "It's all going to these people at the top."

"Tell her to get a lawyer," I advised.

"I did."

"What did she say?"

"She said she would handle it."

I checked my phone, pretending that I got a text. "I have to go," I said, reading the names of apps on the screen.

"Who is that?" Mom asked.

"Peter," I lied. "He wants to get drinks."

"Tell him I said hi." Mom rose to her feet, knowing that our visiting time was over.

I kissed her cheek before leaving. She was a handful, but her heart was in the right place. I knew she was lonely, but I also knew that she was tired of putting up with Dad's crap. She had been right to leave him.

On my way home, I swung by my favorite Greek restaurant. They had a salad and shish kabobs that I liked. It was early, but I was out and it was on my way. Walking into the restaurant, I noticed Ava sitting at one of the tables with a rather plain looking young woman. I considered going up to her to say hello but decided against it.

We were off the clock. Even though we were friendly in the office, we had never spoken to each other outside of work. I was pleased to see that she was enjoying a meal out. I knew that once payroll hit, she would be able to do so much more than she had before.

I hoped she was treating herself, buying shoes or a bag or whatever it was that she wanted but had been so far out of reach. I walked up to the counter and placed my order. It was already made, so all they had to do was dish it out into a to-go container.

I paid for my meal and left, wondering why Ava was coming up so often. After the conversation with my mother and then randomly running into her in the restaurant, it seemed like fate. I shook my head. I was getting romantic in my old age. Ava was just my secretary and I was just her boss. There was no reason to read more into the chance encounter.

Throwing my food onto the passenger seat, I drove home. The day was over already and I hadn't done very much. Checking the email on my phone as soon as I parked, I saw that the banker had reached out. He just wanted me to know how much he appreciated meeting with me that morning, and that he looked forward to working with me in the future.

I crafted an equally professional email, sending it out with the implicit understanding that yes, I was checking email late Saturday afternoon. Letting myself into my house, I kicked my shoes off. It was time for a little relaxation before dinner. The video games were calling.

Chapter 12

Ava

I caught sight of my boss out of the corner of my eye. Feeling rich after depositing my paycheck, I decided to splurge on an evening out. I called up one of my old friends from college, someone I hadn't been able to see since hooking up with Marcus.

She was thrilled at the invitation and we met up at the Olive Pit, a fast-food type Greek restaurant in a trendy part of town. I walked into the place, dressed in one of Mariah's outfits. After trying them all on, I sorted them by professional appearance, style and color. I hung them all up in my tiny closet and spent a good amount of time just admiring them.

There were ten outfits, easily double my wardrobe in a single donation. I picked a short, flirty purple dress and matched it with a pair of suede boots that I had been carting around since before I was homeless. I felt like I had arrived. I was back on my feet and making bank at my swanky new job.

I was out from under Marcus and free to set my own schedule. I had enough money on my debit card to buy groceries and gas, with a little bit left over to spend on fun stuff. It was my first real dinner date in a long time. I was looking forward to seeing Ari, catching up, and filling her in on everything that was going on with me.

We were over the top excited to see each other. As soon as I laid eyes on her, I realized it had been too long. I gave her a hug and we chatted while the server plated our meals. It was a to-go restaurant but they had some tables. The big difference between dine in and take out was that we received our fare on actual porcelain plates.

I got a salad and a chicken kabob. It wasn't too healthy though, because the salad came with fantastic dressing that I poured all over the plate. Ari got a gyro with French fries. She was a tiny little thing and wasn't particularly worried about calories.

"So, you look fabulous," she began, settling into her seat.

"Thanks, you do too," I replied. I decided to neatly skip over the whole homeless escapade. If I could forget the whole thing myself, I would have. "I got a new job."

"That's great. Where are you working?"

"For Brockton Clothing," I shared. "I'm a secretary."

"Oh?" Ari seemed confused. Being a secretary didn't track with my bachelor's degree. "I thought you would have been in broadcasting by now."

"It's a little bit harder to break in than I thought," I allowed. That was true to an extent. It was certainly hard to break into your chosen career when you had to worry about where your next meal was coming from. "I might go back to it, but I'm really enjoying where I work at the moment."

"That's great!"

"What about you? Have you landed on your feet?"

"I'm also not working in our field," she said with a grin. "I've been waiting tables."

I tried not to act too surprised. "That's good work."

"It is," she agreed. "And I'm going to night school."

"What are you studying?"

"I want to get my master's in business," she answered. "And then I was thinking about opening my own restaurant."

"That is not at all journalism," I laughed.

"Not at all," she replied. "But it keeps me busy. I think I was studying journalism because that's what my parents wanted."

Just then, I looked up to see Nate walking in the door. I glanced back down at my salad, almost embarrassed to be caught outside the office. Then I reminded myself that it was Saturday. I wasn't goofing off on the clock, I was having dinner with an old friend.

Nate didn't acknowledge me, so I felt awkward about standing up and saying hello to him. It seemed like we were just going to ignore each other. That was fine. He wasn't exactly a friend, although I did feel like we were getting closer the longer we worked together. Maybe he just didn't see me, I told myself.

Ari saw me looking and leaned over to whisper in confidence, "He's hot."

"That's my boss," I said absently.

"I can see why you like your job," she teased.

I blushed, looking away. The street scene out the window suddenly took on new importance. There were a few cars parked out there and I focused on the way the afternoon sunlight hit their windshields.

"It's not like that," I insisted.

"Okay," she gave up the chase, understanding that I wanted to drop the subject.

It was the first time I really noticed how attractive Nate was. Stopping myself from going down that path, I was reminded of my first impression. I knew he was hot. I had known it from the very beginning. I just forgot after spending so much time with him.

Ari threw it back in my face and I laughed at myself. Of course he was good looking, but he was my boss. I didn't know anything about his love life and it was none of my business. He ordered some food for take out and left, freeing me to breathe normally once again.

I looked over at my friend and saw her watching me carefully. I cleared my throat, stabbing a hunk of chicken and fitting it into my mouth. She couldn't know what Nate and I had been through. That he rescued me from poverty and set me up in an apartment, that he was responsible for the clothes I wore and the money in my bank account. It was all legitimate of course. I wasn't some kind of kept woman. But without Nate, Mariah never would have come into my life. And without Mariah, I would still be sleeping on the streets.

"What ever happened to Marcus?" Ari asked innocently.

I choked on the meat. Just hearing his name set me off.

"That good?" my friend observed as I reached for my water.

Washing the bite down, I composed myself. "We broke up."

"Can I ask why?"

"He was cheating on me," I responded. "I don't really want to talk about it."

"Fair." Ari put a hand up to indicate her capitulation.

We finished our meal talking about other classmates. Ari filled me in on a few of the other girls we ran with. I was delighted to learn how they were doing, and that some of them were already happily married.

"We should do this again sometime," I said as we gathered our things to leave.

"Definitely," Ari agreed. "Don't be such a stranger."

"I won't," I promised.

We hugged before getting into our respective cars. I drove back to my apartment, feeling better than I had in a long time. Life was looking up. The dinner hadn't really cost me that much, so I had plenty more in the budget for other things. I decided to put a thousand dollars away for a living upgrade, but that still left more than a thousand dollars to play with. If I did the same, I would easily be able to afford something on my own in a few months.

I had half a tub of ice cream left over from my party the night before. It was just waiting for me in the freezer. Grabbing a spoon, I sat down to watch an old romantic comedy. The woman was young and beautiful and the man was rich and successful. It almost seemed familiar, as if the story was about me and not some Hollywood starlet. I pushed that thought aside, laughing at my own assumptions.

I spent the rest of the weekend by myself, catching up on all the wonderful things that I hadn't been able to do for so long. I took a bath. The tub wasn't very big, but it was big enough. I found a recipe that I wanted to try, and cooked chicken with vegetables in my own kitchen. I put on some music and danced around my living room. I downloaded a book from the library and sat on the couch for a few hours, losing myself to the characters.

When Monday came around, I was ready to go back to work. Brockman Clothing felt like the anchor in my life. Going to work every day was almost like coming home. I had plenty on my plate, but all of it was doable. I was good at my job, and proud of it.

I dressed in the blue pantsuit. It might have been free, but it was cutting edge. I felt like a new woman. I couldn't remember the last time I wore something that I hadn't found at a thrift store. Even in college, I didn't let myself splurge on clothing. A few pairs of jeans and a few T-shirts were enough to get me through four years of undergraduate studies. When I was dating Marcus, he was the one who picked my outfits.

Wearing Mariah's fashions, I felt like I was owning my own body. She had a sixth sense for my style and figure, and all the choices were flattering. I fit into the office decorum much more efficiently in expensive threads. Riding up in the elevator, I got a bunch of compliments, starting my day off on the right foot.

Nate wasn't in the office when I arrived, which was strange. There was no free breakfast, but that was okay. I wasn't hungry anymore. I packed my own lunch to save a few bucks, but it was full of fun things like fruit and raisins and I was looking forward to digging in later.

I settled into my chair and turned on my computer. There were a bunch of emails to answer. It was obvious that many of the senior staff members were working over the weekend. The time and date stamps let me know that some of them were up at three in the morning, shooting off mass communications that could have waited until the morning. No matter. I responded to everything that required my attention and then began to work on Nate's calendar for the week.

He came in around ten and I stood up to greet him. I wasn't sure whether to offer my hand for a shake or to just smile and nod. Either way, it didn't seem respectful to just ignore him and continue with what I was doing.

"Good morning," I said.

"Good morning," he replied.

"Would you like to go over your schedule?"

"Yes." He opened his door, walking inside without another word.

I grabbed my pen and paper and followed him. "How was your weekend?"

"Fine. Yours?"

"Good," I replied. I didn't want to seem overly excited, but he knew all about my situation. "I spent money like it was going out of style."

"I find that hard to believe." He set his briefcase down beside the desk and opened the curtains.

The office was flooded with light, and I had to blink several times to adjust. "This is the casual office line." I turned slightly so he could see the contours of the clothing I wore.

"It looks good," he said tightly. I wasn't sure if he approved or not so I figured it was time to just get down to business.

"You have two meetings today and a conference call."

"Prep materials?"

"Already in your inbox."

"You're on top of it," he said, finally meeting my eyes.

I gave him a brilliant smile. I didn't care if he was my boss and I didn't care if it was inappropriate, I enjoyed his praise. He gave me the one thing I really needed in life, genuine appreciation. Everything else was optional. Food, shelter, clothing, it was all secondary to actual respect. I felt like I won the jackpot with this job, and I didn't care who knew it.

Returning to my desk, I began sorting through the voice mails. I copied down all the information that people left, putting the messages into emails and sending them to the correct recipients. The messages that were for Nate, I sent in separate communications, each one titled with the caller's name and date-time stamp.

That was what he preferred. He could call them back or answer me and have me call them back. It was easier than just handing him an entire list of messages. It was almost lunch time when my phone buzzed.

Looking down, I found it was a message from Marcus. Damn him. I thought I blocked his ass. Checking the phone number, I saw he was texting from a different phone. Either he bought a new number, or he had borrowed someone else's. Another thought crossed my mind. It was possible he was tuned in to some type of stalking software or an app that allowed him to bypass my block.

I couldn't stop myself from muttering under my breath. Blocking that number too, I turned the phone off. Nate chose that particular moment to come out of his office on his way to the elevator. He stopped, looked over at me, and smiled sardonically.

"Did I just hear you curse?"

"What?" I looked up, mortified. "No. Sorry. Yes. I'm sorry."

"What's wrong?"

"It's my ex-boyfriend," I said without thinking. "I thought I blocked him, but he found some way around it. He texted me from a different number."

"Do you want a new phone?" Nate asked.

I sat stunned, feeling my jaw slide open. He couldn't be offering me a brand new phone. That was above and beyond the call of duty. I couldn't possibly accept the offer, considering that depending on the model, we could be talking about upwards of a thousand dollars.

"It's a business phone," Nate explained. "I meant to get you one anyway."

"But I don't need it for business," I argued.

"Don't tell them that," he advised.

"I can't accept it," I denounced his gift.

"It's not a gift. It's company property and you have to return it when you leave. It's just so I can get in touch with you," Nate explained.

My thoughts racing, I looked down at my desk. Could I really get away with borrowing a new phone from the office? If I just followed Nate's directions and didn't tell IT my personal sob story, they would assume everything was legitimate. If it really was a business phone on loan to company employees, then I wouldn't be putting anyone out of pocket. It wasn't really a magnanimous gesture, just a mutually beneficial work around for my personal problem.

"Okay," I agreed.

"Great," he said. "I'll shoot them an email when I get back."

"Thank you," I called after him.

"Don't thank me," he replied. "Just doing your job is good enough."

I watched the empty hallway as he rode down in the elevator, wondering how I had gotten so lucky. He couldn't know, but the use of a company phone was almost as gratifying as a roof over my head. There was so much I owed to Nate and his family that I could never repay. I poured myself back into my job with renewed enthusiasm. If all he was looking for was a stellar secretary, then I would be the best damned secretary he ever had. I would make all the other secretaries look like scum. I would prove to him that I was worth every last kindness he had bestowed upon me, making it my singular goal in life to do my best for Nate Brockman and his company.

Chapter 13

Nate

I came back from my lunch at the gym. There was a fitness club right down the block and since I spent more time in the office than I did at home, I purchased a membership. When I was really feeling antsy, it helped to go for a quick run, or even a swim, before heading off to my next meeting.

That day, I pounded out a few miles, showered and redressed before walking back to the office. I swung by IT instead of sending an email. Since I was up anyway, it never hurt to show my face. That was one thing I didn't learn from my father. He kept himself hidden away, only interacting with the rest of the staff through Lauren. I was determined not to make the same mistake, and I put it on my calendar to go wandering around the office every few days.

It was a good plan. I would take an hour, stop in and chat with the VPs, and take a look at the designs that were on the slate for the next season. Next, I would show up in the break room to see who was there, make myself a conspicuous cup of coffee and stay to chat. Lastly, I would swing through the accounting department and check in with the accounts receivable folks to see if they were having any problems.

I was able to stay on top of things that way. An issue with a distributor might not rise to the level of an email, but if I was right there, someone might open up. I read all about the technique in some of the many leadership books I purchased. I wanted to make sure that I was doing a good job and that I could hit the ground running. One of the techniques that nearly all the books recommended was to walk the floor and spend time with the employees.

So, I figured I could kill two birds with one stone. I could put in an appearance at IT and make sure that everything was running smoothly from their end. I could also get them started working on a phone for Ava.

By the time I arrived back at my office, there was an email waiting for me. I forwarded it to her and assumed that she would be all over it. At about three that afternoon, she popped into my office to show off her new tech.

It was a sleek black phone with a data plan and a bevy of apps already installed. It had all the office stuff so that she could work on spreadsheets and things from home. It also had voicemail so she could screen out unwanted calls. Of course, the ex-boyfriend wasn't going to get his hands on this number, I was sure of that.

It bothered me that he was stalking her. I didn't know much about him other than a general sense that he was the cause of her recent homelessness. I didn't know how any man could throw a woman out onto the streets. Even someone I didn't like wouldn't deserve that kind of treatment.

If Ava was not destitute when we met, I wouldn't have felt so protective. But seeing as how I had to swoop in and rescue her, I felt some measure of responsibility. The guy was a complete trash can. If it was up to me, I would counsel her to report him to the police, but I didn't know if that suggestion would be appreciated.

Knowing my mother's nonprofit like I did, I understood that they were on the lookout for such things. Ava presented herself originally as a single woman, someone unencumbered by previous relationships. That wasn't exactly true. A business cell phone was the least I could do. In all honesty, I had considered ordering one for her a week ago, it had just slipped my mind.

"Ava," I said seriously, breaking through her excited chit chat about the phone.

"Yes?"

"You would tell me if something else was wrong." I meant it as a question, but it came out more like a command.

She pressed her lips together, considering my request. "Of course."

"If you see him…" I warned.

"I'll let you know," she promised.

"Okay." I let the matter drop.

Silence fell, heavy and awkward between us. I had overstepped a boundary and I knew it. My demand wasn't exactly professional. It wasn't romantic either, but lay somewhere along the lines of concern. I wanted to impress upon her the seriousness of her situation. I heard too many stories from my mother about women who underestimated the fury of their domestic partners.

Yes, I wanted her around to work for me, but I also wanted to make sure she was safe. It wasn't completely selfish and she knew it. She gave me a small smile before walking back to her desk and shutting the door behind her.

I cursed out loud, throwing my pen across the room. I was getting way too involved in her business. She was just an employee and I needed to remain unemotional. Giving her a phone, a new wardrobe and an apartment was fine, as long as I knew where to draw the line. I couldn't let myself get carried away. I reminded myself that she was off limits.

I had plenty of women that I could call up to satisfy my craving for sex. Jill, for starters, was always available and interested. There were also Cherry and Amanda. They were each fun in their own way. I would have to give one of them a call tonight if I was going to maintain my distance from Ava. She was fast becoming the first person I thought of when I woke up in the morning and the last face I imagined before calling it a night.

The clock was ticking away toward five when Ava knocked on the door again.

"Come in!" I called.

She pushed the door open and I saw my father in the foyer just behind her. I couldn't stop my head from dropping back in frustration. It was a small movement, but it didn't go unnoticed. If I was playing a high stakes game of poker, I would have just announced my losing hand. Luckily, my dad didn't care.

He barged right in as if he owned the place, nearly shoving Ava out of the way. I made eye contact with my Ava, apologizing to her. She was distracted and didn't notice the subtle communication. Then the door slammed shut and Dad was walking toward the window.

He paused to look out on the city, surveying the domain that had once belonged to him. "Hot secretary," he said offhandedly.

"Stay away from her," I commanded, searching for the force necessary to back up the request.

It almost seemed like a futile gesture. Either my father was going to hit on Ava or he wasn't. He wouldn't listen to me. And unfortunately, this was one chauvinistic bastard that I couldn't protect her from. Short of getting into a fistfight with the old man, nothing else would work. I had never hit him, although I had come close. After what he did to Mom, not to mention the bevy of women he slept with over the years, I couldn't summon any more outrage.

"Nice desk," Dad looked down at the substandard pine that served as my workstation. "What happened to the old one?"

"I burned it," I said.

"Really?"

"Not really. It's in storage."

"Well, get it out. I liked that thing."

"You can have it," I said. "Take it, please. No one else wants to touch it."

He narrowed his eyes, trying to decide if I was joking. "Call the VPs, let's have a working lunch."

"It's almost five," I said.

"A working dinner then," he continued, unwilling to give up.

"Is there something you want?" I shoved my hands in my pockets, feeling like a teenager again.

"I just want to check up on you," he said.

"Don't."

"You're not too big for your father to help, are you?" He jokingly gave me a one-two punch, as if I was still a kid and I cared about that sort of thing.

"I'm really busy," I lied.

"Alright, well I'll ask that secretary out for a drink." He turned to walk away.

"No!" I snapped. "Leave her alone."

Lex Brockton stopped, turned, and favored me with the ugliest smile I had ever seen. "You like her."

"I don't," I insisted.

"You do," he challenged, taking another step back toward my desk. "If you don't, then she's still on the market."

"Okay fine," I snapped. "I like her. I'm going to ask her out. Don't touch her."

"You've got good taste in women," he approved, turning back to the door. "Come by my house sometime. Don't be a stranger."

"Okay," I responded, relieved that I had managed to usher him out the door without too much drama.

I didn't even want to imagine what a dinner meeting with all the VPs would have been like. It would have been torture for everyone involved except my father. No one would know who was in charge of the meeting, and there would have been plenty of awkward pauses and unflattering jokes. No one would want to go, but everyone would show up out of obligation. I would be forced to suffer through story after story about how great the company was a year ago when my father was the CEO. And everyone would expect me to shut the thing down after a half hour so they could all get home to their wives.

A short time later, I was in no mood for Jonas' call when it came in, and I considered asking Ava to take a message. But the threat the younger man represented made me think twice. I couldn't let my daddy issues get in the way of making the right decision for the company. I didn't want to earn an enemy just because my father got under my skin.

I gave Ava the go ahead to transfer the call, noting that there was only half an hour left in her workday. Jonas was over the top friendly as usual, flattering me with his signature brand of charm.

"Hard at work or hardly working?" he asked jokingly.

"You know me," I refused to comment.

"Listen, smart guy like you, anyone would be thrilled to pick your brain. How about you and me, sushi? You pick the time and the place. I won't take no for an answer."

What could I say? The guy wasn't going to let me go without a fight, and I wasn't even sure if I wanted him to. He could very well be the next FUBU and all he was asking for was an hour of my time. I agreed to meet him but was able to push the meeting to the following week. That gave me some time to work up to it, knowing that the entire affair was likely to be a headache.

Ava came into the office at five on the dot to ask if there was anything else she could do for me before clocking out. I stared at her without speaking, my eyes narrowed under duress. It seemed like everything that could have possibly gone wrong in the past hour had gone wrong. It was as if a small tornado blew through my office, upsetting the potted plants and blowing out the windows. I was left to pick up the pieces and I didn't want to do it alone.

"I need you to work on a project," I said.

She shifted back on her heels, uncomfortable under the power of my gaze. I never asked her to work late before. I never stared at her as if she were meat on a stick. Yet I found myself doing both and not feeling even the slightest bit of remorse.

Chapter 14

Ava

After listening to Nate blow hot air my direction, I went back to my desk in a huff. I told myself that he was the boss. If he wanted me to finish a project before I left for the night, that was his prerogative. I couldn't shake the notion that he was just making up work for me to do. I felt like I stepped into the office at the wrong time and he was lashing out at me for something someone else had said.

I shook my head to clear it. I was a professional. If he was being a dick, that was his problem. I would put in another hour to finish what he wanted done and then just leave. I didn't have to worry about missing dinner at the shelter or catching the bus or even walking down the street in the dark.

I splurged for a parking spot with part of my first paycheck, so I was covered as far as transportation was concerned. Nate asked me to clear his calendar for the rest of the night. I didn't know what he was talking about since it was the end of the day. But I didn't want to argue. He seemed like he would bite my head off, so I just got out of there as quickly as possible.

Checking his calendar, I saw there were still two more meetings. It was my own bias that caused me to think the workday was over. Of course, he didn't clock out at five. He wasn't an hourly employee but the CEO of the entire company. He met with people on their schedules, which sometimes meant video calls as late as eight or nine in the evening.

It was too close to the appointed hour to send emails or simply cancel the meeting over web-based software. I put in a call to the secretaries of the two people he was supposed to meet with. Apologizing for unforeseen problems, I managed to reschedule both for later in the week.

That done, I wasn't sure what else to do. I tinkered with the expense reports, making sure that all the columns added up. I highlighted a few areas and added some extra text explaining some expenditures. It would be easier for the finance team to categorize things that way. Other than that, I didn't really have a lot of work to do.

I did some online snooping that I supposed technically could count as work. I looked Brockman Clothing up on social media to see what kinds of things they were posting. It was all pretty bland. They announced the sales that were happening and there were a few congratulatory posts about people moving up in the company. There didn't appear to be any personality to the brand, just pictures of products and smiling, happy workers.

I played an online word game, flexing my mental muscles until the clock struck six. I looked at Nate's door, wondering what I should do. If I just left, would he be upset? If I went in to ask him for permission, would he deny me again? I decided to err on the side of caution and opened the door once more.

Inside, Nate had turned the light on. He was staring at his computer as if the meaning of life was written across the screen. I figured it was probably stock reports that had him so engaged. Either that, or he was watching porn. I couldn't see because the display was facing away from me.

"I cleared your schedule," I said.

"Thank you," he replied.

"I'm going home now," I added.

"Okay."

I let myself out, feeling relieved. I managed to tiptoe past the sleeping ogre without consequence. I could leave the building without angering my boss and one extra hour in the office didn't present that much of a hardship.

I wondered what had gotten under Nate's skin. Maybe it was his father. I had never seen him act so surly, but I had never met his father either. I couldn't imagine anyone not being head over heels in love with Mariah. She was a breath of fresh air, so beautiful and energetic. Whoever Lex Brockman was, he had the audacity to throw away the woman who had saved my life. On the basis of that alone, I realized I might hate him.

Maybe Nate felt the same way. Maybe he was pissed that his father disrespected his mom. Maybe that's why he was in such a foul mood. I was sure that if I found myself between two warring loved ones, I might feel similarly unhappy.

Still, he didn't have to take it out on me. I didn't like the way he looked at me when I went in to ask him if I could leave. It was a hungry look, one that told me he considered deepening our relationship. Men didn't look at employees that way. That look was reserved for wives or mistresses, girlfriends, prostitutes or pin ups. I had seen that look before, though not in Nate's eyes. I knew it meant trouble.

I drove home and parked on the street, walking up the stairs to my new home. Once inside, I kicked off my heels, slipped out of my blouse and undid my fly. Releasing myself entirely from the shackles of the day, I debated whether to take a shower or not. I just wanted to feel free. I wanted to leave the confusion and frustration behind and hide under the covers until daybreak.

Climbing into bed, I closed my eyes. The first thing that came to me was Nate's face. He sat behind his desk like some sort of evil genius. His suit was impeccable, his tie perfectly arranged, the entire ensemble tailor made. He clasped his hands in front of his chest the way he had done before I left.

My pulse quickened, and I realized with horror that I was actually turned on by his boorish attention. He opened the door to something illicit, something I never should have seen. He might be saying all the right things and playing the part of a respectful boss, but he had shown me his hand. Right in the center, where the king should be, was a joker. It was only a matter of time before he played it.

I felt my heart beat in my throat, envisioning that day. Would I have the courage to turn him away? Or would I fall into his bed as easily as I walked into his office? I would have to be careful. There were laws governing relationships in the workplace. I couldn't afford to fall in love with my boss, and he couldn't afford to fall in love with me. That was, of course, if love was even on the table.

Chapter 15

Nate

I went home that night and had a little too much to drink. It was horrible dealing with my father. He was such a bull, rampaging through everyone else's lives with no consideration. I liked to think of myself as a capable and even-tempered person, but Lex pushed my buttons like no one else could.

When Ava came into my office later to let me know she was leaving, I didn't think anything of it. It wasn't until the next morning that I realized I had kept her past five. She had rescheduled the late-night meetings like I asked her to, but she didn't need to stay past her shift to do that. I had been so focused on my own drama that I forgot to think about others.

There was a bigger problem and that was I had allowed myself to consider Ava as more than just a secretary. Her presence in my life grew larger by the day. One moment I was sharing breakfast with her and the next my parents were hinting that we should get together. I wasn't used to one woman monopolizing so much space in my mind and it made me uneasy.

Staring at her in my office, I allowed myself to think about what it might be like to kiss her. I imagined taking her by the arm and pulling her in tight. I would grasp the back of her skull and feast on her lips, leaving no room for argument. She might be surprised, but when she understood what was happening, she would open herself up to it.

That was as far as I got before my rational brain cut me off. I texted Cecilia, a friend of a friend who had indicated some interest. We arranged to meet for drinks. Unfortunately, I got too much of a head start on my own and I had to cancel. I swore that I would make it up to her, but she seemed upset.

I climbed into my hot tub and stared up at the ceiling, doing essentially nothing until I got cold. Afterwards, I went back downstairs and played some games until one in the morning. I had to be up at the crack of dawn and I didn't have it in me to call in sick. Against my better judgment, I hauled myself to bed.

It was hard to shut my brain off. I got maybe three hours of sleep before I had to get up again. At this rate, my father's interest in the business was going to kill me. I couldn't let him get into my head like this. If a simple visit resulted in a poor night's sleep, what would a full-fledged argument do? I chewed some vitamins and chased them with coffee.

I needed to talk to someone, but I didn't know who. I texted Peter before leaving for work, asking him if he wanted to grab lunch. He answered quickly and I was relieved when he agreed. He was the best friend I had at the moment. He wasn't a family member and he wasn't a rival. He knew my entire history and I could trust him not to go running to the board if I admitted to some tiny emotional issue.

In my office, I waited for Ava to join me. She always came in for breakfast, even though she was capable of buying her own. It was a ritual we began when she was first hired and one that I enjoyed. We talked over the schedule and I was able to get settled before my work began. But she didn't come in that day.

I waited for fifteen minutes before checking for her in the reception area. She was there, behind her desk, reading her emails. She heard the door open and turned to face me as I leaned out, wondering where she was.

"Are you going to have breakfast?" I asked.

"I had breakfast already," she said.

"Have another breakfast," I commanded, leaving the door open and walking away.

She appeared momentarily, looking a little miffed but mostly congenial. She reached for a croissant and a napkin, grabbing me one as well. Bringing them to the desk, she set them down before going back to fetch the coffee. Once it was all arranged, we sat together like normal.

I knew what was wrong. She was upset that I made her stay late the previous night. Whether or not I had been out of line, I couldn't have her acting like that. She was my secretary and I was her boss. If I needed her to put in some extra hours, that came with the job. I wanted to let her know that she had better get over herself. It wasn't like I had made an inappropriate gesture or asked her to do anything unreasonable.

"I'm sorry I asked you to stay late yesterday," I began.

"It's fine," she replied.

"That may happen occasionally."

"I understand."

Since the old business was concluded, I moved straight on to the new business. "What's on the schedule for today?"

"You have several meetings," she said before checking her note pad. "A one o'clock with Mr. Clark from footwear, a three o'clock with the sales team in Italy and a five o'clock with your mother."

"She made an appointment?" I asked.

"Apparently," Ava replied. "I may have let it slip that your father was in here yesterday."

"Oh."

"She insisted on alerting you that she was coming."

"She doesn't have to wait until five."

"She had some appointments herself." Ava lowered her chin to take a bite of her croissant and I saw a flash of cleavage underneath her shirt.

There was something else on her shoulder, a bright red patch of skin. I wondered if it was a birthmark or maybe a tattoo that had been removed. Either way, it wasn't any of my business. I diverted my eyes before I got caught.

"Do you think I should just toss them out?" I asked suddenly. Forget waiting for my lunch with Peter, I could unload a little bit of my anxiety on

Ava. After everything I had given her, I felt like she owed me a sympathetic ear.

"Who? Your parents?"

"Yeah, both of them."

Ava smiled and I saw that with that one question she forgave me all my sins. "You're in a tight spot. Not that I know anything about it. But all along your parents were in charge, not just of you but of everyone around you. Now that's changed and I don't think they realize it."

"Maybe I need to help them realize it," I suggested.

"I guess you could talk to them."

"Maybe *you* should talk to them," I shot back, waiting to see how she would react.

She crossed her arms over her lovely chest and gave me a look that would melt steel. "I can do a lot of things as your secretary, but getting your parents to leave you alone isn't one of them."

"What are the other things you can do as my secretary?" I asked before I could stop myself.

"I can order lunch," she said, not taking the bait. "I can rearrange your files. I can book you a trip to Cancun."

"Can you book my parents a trip to Cancun?" I muttered.

"I can," she replied, "but you'll have to tell them about it."

"That doesn't help."

"Do you want me to tell her you're busy?"

"No, I'll handle it." I turned my attention to the computer screen, signaling that our breakfast chat was over. "Will you block off an hour over lunch? I'm meeting with Peter from product design."

"Sure," she agreed, cleaning up our little picnic before walking out the door. I watched her leave with more enthusiasm than I should have. Her butt was packaged neatly into the pants she wore, an added bonus for any male coworkers. I decided to keep Ava on the list of staff to try on new designs. It would make for an interesting fashion show in my own office.

Peter came up around noon and we went out for pizza. I was finally able to vent about my father and all his bullshit. I really wanted to explain how messed up his visit made me, how I couldn't sleep, and found myself drinking a few too many too fast.

"Calm down," Peter said, taking a bite of his slice. "Everyone knows your old man is a handful. I'm surprised you handle him as well as you do."

"Thanks. I think."

"Give him a few months. He'll go away on his own."

"I'm not sure that he will," I said. "He wanted me to get all you guys together to have a dinner meeting."

"God, that sounds awful." Peter frowned.

"I didn't let him get out of the gate on that one," I assured.

"Thank you."

"Maybe you should make a Lex Brockton employee of the year award or something like that. Something that gives him an excuse to come back to the office once." Peter took a sip from his soda, grabbing a French fry and waving it around. "We'll have a catered lunch and let him give someone a plaque and put him in charge of the whole thing. He'll figure out that he likes to be retired and go away happily."

"That's not a bad idea," I mused.

"Thank you."

"No, really. It's like promoting someone to get them out of your hair. No one can argue, and the problem is solved without any drama."

"Exactly."

"I'll have Ava work on that when I get back."

"Speaking of Ava, how is she?" Peter asked.

I sighed. I didn't really want to talk about Ava. I didn't know how I felt about her. Other than a vague uneasiness around the fact that I was thinking about her far too often, there was really nothing to say.

"We're getting along. She's a hard worker and I haven't been able to find fault with anything she's done yet."

"What about your old secretary?" Peter asked.

"Shannon?" I guessed.

"Was that her name?"

I shrugged. "She went back into the pool when I got promoted, I think. She was nice, she just wasn't executive material."

"You didn't want to bring her along for the ride?" He eyed my slice after finishing his own, and I pushed it toward him.

"Why are we talking so much about my secretaries?" I asked, offended. "What's happening with your secretary?"

"Nothing." Peter shrugged, helping himself to what was left of my pizza. "But I'm married."

"So was my father," I mumbled.

"Point taken."

We finished up our lunch and walked back to the office together. I went into one meeting after another until five o'clock when my mother showed up. She and Ava passed each other in the hall. I let Ava go instead of asking her to stick around and entertain my mom.

"I like that dress on Ava," Mom commented as she walked in.

"Don't," I said.

"Don't what?" she feigned ignorance.

"Just don't."

"Sweetheart, just because your father is a bastard —excuse my language —doesn't mean you are. You don't have a wife and a child, and you're not a serial cheater."

"She's my secretary," I replied, trying to put an end to the discussion.

"And she's a woman, and you like her," Mom said.

"Can we talk about something else?" I asked.

"What would you like to talk about?"

I stroked my chin, thinking about my conversation with Peter. He mentioned throwing my dad a bone, but I didn't see why it wouldn't also work for my mother. "I was thinking about having a prize. Something like the best dressed Mariah Harris Couture prize. You could arrange it all. It would be an annual affair you could hold at the country club or something."

She frowned, taken aback by my suggestion. It wasn't an insult or an inappropriate proposal, but somehow, she smelled something shady. "Okay," she said reluctantly.

"You can get together with Ava for everything you need," I continued, ushering her toward the door.

"Okay." This time she seemed a little more excited, as if she was letting herself get familiar with the idea.

"I'm thinking May for the spring fashion line." I put my hand on her shoulder, opening up the door.

"That doesn't give me a lot of time," she said.

"It would mean a lot to the company," I replied.

"Okay." She tipped forward to give me a peck on the cheek and walked out of the office without bothering me any further.

I watched her go, in awe of my friend Peter. First his suggestion about open interviews landed me Ava and now he had handed me a surefire way to get out from under my parents. I had to hand it to him, he was a genius.

On Friday, I felt like things were going smoothly with Ava. She joined me for breakfast every day without prodding. She was quick with a smile and seemed relaxed in my presence. I was relaxing too, although I caught myself staring at her chest more than once.

"Hey, why don't you come out with me?" I asked over bagels and cream cheese on Friday morning. She didn't respond, so I continued just to make sure she understood that I wasn't asking her out on a date. "I have to meet Jonas for sushi after work. We could make it a working dinner and come up with an excuse to ditch him early."

She grinned. "I think the best part of drinks with Jonas would be ditching him."

"So you'll come?"

"I don't know," she hesitated. "I don't have anything to wear."

"Wear what you have on," I suggested. It wasn't exactly a clubbing outfit, but we weren't going to a rave. For drinks with a fellow trust fund baby, understated was the way to go. "Come on, it'll be fun."

"Okay," she relented. "But only if you let me make up the excuse."

I gave her a curious look. What did she mean, make up the excuse? "What are you going to say?"

"Mmm," she considered, turning up her button nose. "That my dog is desperately sick and we need to pick him up and take him to the vet."

"That's good. What about, a pipe burst in my basement?" I tried.

"Why would *I* have to leave to deal with your pipe?" she shot me down.

"Why would *I* have to leave to deal with your dog?" I challenged.

"The office," we said at once.

"There's an emergency at the office," I elaborated.

"We're being raided by the FBI."

I shook my head. "No. He can look that up. There's a problem with payroll or something that demands both of our attention."

"Okay," she relented. "But mine is more exciting."

"And also illegal," I pointed out.

We went straight from the office to the restaurant, and what started out as a good idea rapidly disintegrated into something more frustrating than I had expected. I forgot all about how Jonas treated Ava the first time they met. He was all over her and I had to scrape him off.

It was the same, but only worse in a casual situation. We walked up, arm in arm, not actually together, but close enough to give any normal man pause. Jonas blew right through it, whisking

Ava away to show her where you could stand to watch the sushi being made.

I sat at the table, trying not to let it get to me. The man was an idiot. There was no way Ava was into him. She looked like she was having a good time, though. Maybe there was something to the overly enthusiastic, good-natured kid. It was the same thing that was likely to catapult him to fame and fortune once he picked a designer and got all his ducks in a row.

I didn't want to compete with him on the corporate battlefield, but I sure as hell was going to get in his way if he continued to hit on my secretary. I was about to butt in when Ava extracted herself from the viewing station and found me again.

"Help me," she whispered.

I smiled. I was right all along; she wasn't impressed by Jonas's fake charm. Standing up, I tracked him down, throwing an arm over his shoulder and leading him to the table. We placed our order, including a few drinks. We talked about Jonas's new venture and I fought to ignore the way he salivated over Ava.

I knew Ava wasn't my date. She was my employee. She was just here because I asked her to come, not because there was anything romantic between us. She also seemed to be doing a fine job of keeping Jonas's wandering fingers at bay. He would reach out to caress her knee and she would gently move aside to avoid him. He would pat her hand and she would return the gesture with a little more force, driving home the fact that she was unavailable.

After about half an hour, I had enough. I checked my email, pretending to get a message from HR. "Oh, there's a problem with payroll. It looks like Ava and I will have to go."

"I'm sure you can deal with it yourself," Jonas said, his eyes focused on Ava.

"I have to go too," she excused herself. "It's a cumbersome process that takes multiple people."

"Well, I'm sorry to hear that." Jonas stood up to say goodbye. "You have to come to our next meeting. I'm sure I can think of a salary to entice you away from my man." He jabbed me with a fake right hook, pretending to be kidding when he really wasn't. I could see in his eyes that he would definitely headhunt Ava if I let him.

I wasn't going to get into a bidding war with him. I made our excuses and she was on my side. We detached ourselves from his many tentacles and walked swiftly to the door. Out on the sidewalk, Ava collapsed into a fit of laughter. It felt good to know that we were on the same page and that she wouldn't be jumping ship. Still, the way he was breathing all over her made my blood boil. He wasn't good enough for Ava. Even though I had no claim, I didn't think anyone else was either.

Chapter 16

Ava

It felt like we were two cat burglars fleeing the scene of the crime. I was drunk off that one glass of wine and the excitement of the evening out. It had been a long time since I had dinner with friends and even though neither man I was with technically qualified as a friend, Nate was pretty close.

I didn't like Jonas, but I didn't think he was dangerous. He kept trying to touch me and I kept having to push him off. But at no point did I feel unsafe or like he would try anything truly objectionable. If I was his secretary, I might have cause to be alarmed. I almost laughed in his face when he offered me a job. He probably would pay more than Nate, but I was equally sure I didn't want to look at the job description.

Outside on the street, I slid my arm around Nate's, unable to stop myself from laughing. It felt so good to have an accomplice. The lie went off exactly as we planned, with Jonas none the wiser. Our cars were parked side by side in a parking garage across the street. The night was young and the air was sweet.

The fact that I shouldn't be so familiar with my boss was lost on me at that moment. I allowed him to walk me across traffic and into the parking structure. We separated when we reached our cars. I had my key fob in my hand when he said something. I turned because I didn't hear him well and found him right beside me.

"If you ever get a job offer from Jonas, let me know," he said.

I laughed. I wasn't sure what he was doing so close, but I wasn't afraid. We were partners in crime, about to call it a night. Pretty soon I would be comfortably ensconced in my own living room, dressed in my pajamas, watching old romantic comedies. Why then did I feel a quickening of my pulse?

"I can't get you out of my mind," Nate said.

Before I knew what was happening, he leaned forward, slipping a hand up underneath my hair to cradle the back of my head. He pressed his lips to mine, the suddenness of the embrace taking my breath away.

I didn't know what to do with my hands. They were limp by my sides, then awkward weights between us. I tried to focus on the connection, but my head was spinning. I felt my feet lifting up off the ground and I floated in a haze of excitement and confusion.

Just as quickly as he came on, he backed off. He dropped his hand from the base of my skull, stepping away as if he was shocked by his own advance. I licked my lips, tasting the ghost of his brandy and the expensive aroma of his cologne. My lips tingled slightly, a result of his five o'clock shadow. I stared at him without reservation, wondering what would come next.

"I'm sorry," he said.

I couldn't process sorry. Was he sorry for kissing me? Why had he done it then? Was it because I was his secretary? Or because he saw Jonas hitting on me? Was it because I had been too familiar with him in the restaurant and out on the street? Had I somehow crossed a line I wasn't supposed to cross?

He walked away, back to his car. I followed him with my eyes, my feet unresponsive. It looked like he was about to drive off. How could he kiss me like that, with all the pent-up passion of a shipwrecked sailor and then just drive away as if nothing happened? I opened my mouth to demand an explanation but shut it half a second later. I didn't know what the hell to say. Or feel.

"I'm sorry," he said again. "I shouldn't have done that. I'll see you on Monday."

I stood in shock as he climbed behind the wheel and sped away. My feet came unglued finally when his car disappeared. I cursed out loud, getting into my car and slamming the door. After a moment, I began to laugh. There were worse things than being kissed by a generous, attractive man. He might very well have crossed a line, but it took two to tango.

Chapter 17

Nate

I drove home with the pedal to the floor. The whole time I was thinking what an idiot I was. There would have to be damage control. She couldn't think that I would risk her job and my reputation just for one kiss. She also couldn't think that I would take it any further. I was in control of myself, dammit. I didn't act without thinking and I didn't allow myself to get carried away.

It was a fluke. I had been thinking about her with Jonas and I became possessive. I wondered what it would be like to taste her and I satisfied my curiosity. Now I knew, so I didn't have to do it again.

It didn't help that everyone in my life seemed to be pushing us together. Mom, Dad, even Peter, were all making suggestions that I should become involved with Ava as more than just coworkers. Although I didn't value any of those opinions, all for different reasons, it became like a cacophony of voices all clamoring for the same thing.

I didn't want to be unprofessional. I didn't want to make a move on my secretary. I just didn't want her to date anyone else. Was that so unreasonable? I would agree to keep my hands to myself if she would agree to remain celibate for the rest of her life. It sounded like a fair trade off to me.

As soon as I got home, I hit the gym. Punching the bag, I scored higher than I ever had before. I guess I had some aggression I needed to get out. It wasn't working, however. By the end of the session, I still had the same knot in my chest and the same dangerous energy running through my veins.

I decided to call one of my hook ups and get my resolution that way. I invited Tracy over to my place and she showed up. It was fun and it took the edge off, but I found myself still thinking about Ava. I didn't invite Tracy to spend the night and she took the hint. Afterwards, I felt even worse.

How could I keep all these girls on the line without committing to any one of them? I was more like my father than I cared to admit. Going to bed that night, I wondered if I would ever get some relief. I knew exactly what I needed to do and I wasn't interested in doing it. I had to have Ava. But she was off the table. I couldn't risk the fallout.

Drifting off to sleep, I remembered her reaction to my kiss. She was surprised, but more than willing. I tried to forget about it, but knew I never would. Come Monday, I would have to broach the subject. That wasn't a conversation I was looking forward to.

###

The rest of the weekend passed quickly. I went to the club to play some golf. I stopped by my mother's apartment to see how she was doing with the project I had given her. I dodged my father's phone calls, and I put Jonas off again.

I answered some emails and worked out in my home gym. I went for a jog in a city famous for its runners. While I've never competed in a marathon, that didn't make me a slouch. I drove by Ava's place, just by accident on Saturday afternoon and wondered how she was doing.

By Monday, I was itching for another flirtatious conversation. It wasn't fair. The woman who was fast becoming something slightly more than my employee was the one person I couldn't take advantage of. I had to think about things from her perspective. She couldn't afford to anger me since I was paying her. She also relied on me for her housing and her wardrobe, although not directly.

I got into work early, before she clocked in, and ordered breakfast for the two of us. She showed up right on time, as usual, and came into my office to partake of the food. I tried to psyche myself up to have the conversation.

Ava, I would say. *We have to talk.*

She might respond with something casual like, *I had a great time on Friday night.*

To which, I would answer, *We can't ever do that again.*

But for some reason, the words got caught in my throat. The conversation went naturally to what was on the agenda for the day. I had a few meetings, as usual. I planned to walk around the building and check up on my employees. Beyond that, the quarterly reports were due to the stockholders and I had to sign off on them.

There just didn't seem to be time to get into the nitty gritty of our budding affair. She didn't seem uncomfortable and she didn't ask me to explain. In fact, she acted like she was perfectly happy not talking about it, which was a relief. I thought I sensed some reservation on her part, as if the kiss was an aberration and not one worth mentioning.

I tried not to let it bother me. If she had been anxious to discuss its meaning, I would have found myself tongue tied. I wasn't sure how I would handle the accusation first thing in the morning. But she was professional, if a little cold. She learned her lesson about breakfast and submitted to that ritual with tact. But her heart wasn't in it, I could tell. Something had changed subtly, and I knew without asking that there was no going back.

I concentrated on my work for the remainder of the day, although I asked her into my office more than usual. I just wanted to see her, to check if things really were as messed up between us as I thought. Every time she came in, she was perfectly professional. She didn't ask what I was up to, or why I needed so much attention that day.

She gave me the information I asked for each time and politely resisted the urge to communicate further. It drove me crazy. I wanted to see some kind of recognition in her eyes, some longing or frustration, anything but the blank slate that she presented. I wanted to know that I touched her; I wanted to see her reaction—no matter what it was. But she foiled me at every turn.

By the end of the day, I was livid. I started off determined to confront her and tell her that we couldn't possibly see each other outside of the office. Each successive time I asked her to come in, that thought drifted further and further from my mind.

I wanted her. I needed to have her. Nothing was going to stand in my way. I felt the primal instincts rise up inside my chest and they would not be ignored. I watched my rational mind recede until there was nothing left and the only thing that mattered was my wounded ego.

When Ava came back the last time to ask if I needed anything before she went home, I made my move. I stood up from my desk, closing the distance between us. In my gut, logic demanded that I put a stop to this. A denial was on my lips. I was about to tell her that it wasn't working out, that I needed her help to avoid turning this working relationship into a torrid love affair.

She raised her chin, watching me come with grim determination. I was almost there, almost level with her, when she opened her mouth to speak. She caught me off guard with her soft accusation.

"Why did you apologize to me on Friday night?"

That was it. She destroyed the last of my will power with that one simple question. Throwing caution right out the door, I gathered her into my arms and kissed her.

Chapter 18

Ava

It was difficult to remain in the same office with him when he refused to acknowledge what he had done. I wasn't some high school intern or anyone else that he had to refuse. I was a grown woman capable of making up my own mind about who I wanted to date.

If he was lording my position over my head, making me perform sex acts to get a raise, that would be one thing. But he was becoming almost my friend and my confidant. That he also happened to be my boss was irrelevant in some ways. I knew it wouldn't look good, and that we would have to keep our tryst a secret, but so what? Plenty of people snuck around in order to be with the ones they loved. It didn't make what they were doing criminal.

But Nate refused to meet my eyes when I went in to have breakfast with him. He refused to bring up the kiss and focused entirely on the company's business. I couldn't help but feel rejected. Not only would he not face up to what he had done, but he wanted to sweep it under the rug. If that's how he was playing it, I thought, fine by me. I could be just as stubborn and professional as he could.

We got to the end of the day without incident, although he did call me into his office more often than usual. Every time, I wondered if this would be it. Would he bring up the kiss and explain why he tried to pretend it didn't happen? But he never did. I was fed up and ready to go home when the workday ended.

Marching into his office, I was prepared to offer my assistance for any last little tasks he wanted done. What I wasn't prepared for was his sudden capitulation. He stood up, leaving his work at his desk. Coming close, I couldn't think what else he wanted other than a replay of Friday night's action.

I stopped him when he was just a breath away, asking him the question that had been on my mind from the beginning. "Why did you apologize to me on Friday night?"

He didn't answer, but he didn't have to. Without any further drama, he circled my waist with one hand and pulled me in close. I tilted my head up, ready, willing, and able to accept his kiss.

He didn't disappoint. His lips were hard and insistent. He was through playing games.

This time I was ready for him. Instead of holding my arms awkwardly by my sides, I looped them around his neck, falling into the embrace. I opened my mouth, welcoming him inside. It was such a treat to feel him explore my intimate spaces. I felt like this exchange was weeks in the making. Ever since I first laid eyes on him, I knew I wanted to make out with him. He was just too attractive, too powerful, and seductive.

I knew that somewhere within him, he was hoping I would refuse. He didn't want to be known as an office cad or a womanizer like his father. But that wasn't my responsibility. I wanted him, and I wasn't going to stand on ceremony.

I relaxed against him, lengthening my torso as the exchange stoked my fire. He stood rigid, not moving, his entire focus on the kiss. I could feel his chest, rock hard and unforgiving, against my breasts. I wanted to run my fingers across it, to feel the rise and fall of his pectoral muscles. But I didn't dare move away. I was terrified that if I closed my mouth, if I tried to advance the agenda, he would stall me.

He was at war with himself, I could tell. On one hand, he wanted this as badly as I did. But on the other, he was desperately trying to salvage the situation. I decided there was only one way to move forward. I was going to have to shock him into action.

Lowering my arms from around his neck, I went straight for the gold mine. I undid his trousers, my lips firmly pressed to his, my chest rubbing against him. Slipping a hand inside, I wrapped my fingers around his shaft.

He gasped, pulling away and holding me at arm's length. My hand slid from the confines of his pants, leaving the smooth surface of his cock far behind. I licked my lips, ready for more. I wasn't going to make this easy for him. If he wanted to turn me away, he was going to have to do it with a swollen tool. I looked down to see the protrusion beneath his waistline. The pants hung open, his underwear making a tent in the open space.

He growled in frustration, making that split second decision that I hoped he would make. I had done it. I achieved my goal and ripped the Band-Aid off. He was no longer concerned with propriety or how this would look to other people. It was only him and me in the room, and all bets were off.

He came back to me, more adamant than before. He brushed the hair from my face, capturing my lips with an urgency that defied all odds. I reached for his pants again, but he leaned out of the way. I supposed that after crossing that barrier, he wanted to be in control. I slid my hands around to the opposite side of his waist, giving in. Pulling him tight, I lost myself in the kiss, knowing that it was only the beginning.

There was a living room set at the far end of the suite. He lured me there, his movements quick but strained. He sat down on the loveseat, pulling me into his lap. I straddled him, my skirt coming up to my thighs. My shoes still on, I settled against his crotch, feeling the bulge in the exact place it was meant to be.

I lowered my lips to his, resuming the kiss. He slid his hands up my thighs to my hips, grasping my underwear at its waistband. I had a momentary flash of embarrassment. I wasn't wearing sexy panties, just the utilitarian cotton variety, but he didn't care. He pulled them down over my ass, dragging the cloth as far down my thighs as it could go.

I felt the intensity in his play and moved to accommodate him. Raising one leg, I allowed him to slide the garment free. Moving the opposite leg, I resettled myself once he flung the thing off onto the couch. My pussy was naked and primed for battle. She settled roughly on top of his rod, one thin layer of fabric the only remaining barrier.

 Nate didn't stop there. He cupped my backside, kneading gently to prove that this encounter was going to be heart stopping. I tilted my head back, thrusting my chest forward. I didn't know why. There was no thought that went into it. I just let my body take over and do what it wanted. My nipples were raw and demanded attention. The dress was uncomfortable; everything felt hot and itchy and I wanted it off as soon as possible.

 Nate understood. He slid his hands up my spine to the clasp at the back of my neck. Undoing the zipper, he peeled the fabric from my skin. I felt the blessed relief of cool air against my flesh. The office was an inferno, and I was about to make love to my boss.

 He tossed the dress away. I didn't care where it landed, but thought I saw it draped over the arm of the sofa. I was naked except for my bra, and my ugly birthmark was on display. He went straight for it, kissing my shoulder where it was discolored and red. I felt my heart soar. He didn't care about the blemish. He was going to kiss all the embarrassment away.

He placed one hand on my hip, grinding his crotch up into mine. With the other hand, he held my upper back, helping himself to my chest. I undid my bra, pulling it off and tossing it aside. He sat, almost fully dressed, his tie tight against his throat. I didn't have time to divest him of any clothing before he bowed his head and began to feast on my chest.

I moaned, running my fingers through his hair. His tongue was gentle and rough at the same time. He licked across my areola, circling the nipple before sucking it into his mouth. I wiggled deliciously, rubbing my heated skin against his package. He tightened his grip on me in response, to the point that I felt trapped between a rock and a hard place.

I was completely nude. If anyone walked in, our activity would be unmistakable. I had to hope that no one would call or stop by unannounced. I wasn't ashamed of what we were doing, but I didn't want to advertise it either.

Also, I desperately wanted to get him out of his clothes. It wasn't fair that he was still fully dressed. I inched my hands beneath his chin and dug a finger into his tie. He pushed my hands away, but I was insistent. How did he think he was going to make love to me with all that fabric between us?

I tried again, this time successful in loosening his cravat. Sliding the silk out between my fingers, I draped it over the arm of the loveseat. He hardly paused in his pursuit of my honor, nibbling at my chest like a wild animal. I let out a shriek, unable to contain myself.

That got his attention. He reared up out of his seat, releasing my breast and pressing a finger to his lips. I wrapped my fingers around my mouth, my eyes wide in apology. He tipped me over onto the couch, so that my back lay against the cushions and my legs were spread wide around him.

He undid his buttons one by one, pulling his shirt off and tossing it aside. His pants were next, and his underwear followed, revealing his monstrous member. I thought it had been large when I grabbed it earlier that afternoon, but devoid of all clothing, it was truly impressive. I couldn't wait to feel it enter my body. I would close around it, lapping at its heels, eager to feel all the euphoria it could bring.

He wasn't done with me yet. Settling down on top of me, he refused to consummate the act. He kissed me on the lips, fisting a hand in my hair to pull my head back. I followed willingly, eager to give him whatever he wanted if only he would finish the job.

He broke the kiss, trailing his tongue down the side of my jaw to my throat. I writhed beneath him, my entire body on fire. He had the hose with which to soothe me, but he held back. I grabbed his shoulders, digging my fingernails into his muscle. It felt just as solid and strong as I had imagined. He gave me a glimpse of his naked form but wouldn't allow me to fully appreciate it. By holding onto my hair, he forced me to look up at the couch and the ceiling in the distance. I could only feel the weight of his perfect body rubbing against mine.

I wanted to recapture my senses, to be able to look at him as he was clearly looking at me. But every time I tried to move my head, there was a tug on my hair that sent shimmers of discomfort down my spine. So I arched toward him, pressing my chest and my hips up, begging for release.

It worked. He let go, gliding his hand down the side of my body from my breast to my waist. I was able to see him, to drink in the beauty that he represented. His shoulders were solid, so well defined that I thought he must spend all of his off time in the gym. His chest sloped down towards his abdomen, cut like the finest Greek statue. I knew he was fit, but I didn't know he was perfect.

I traced the line of his collarbone from where it began at his throat to where it disappeared under his shoulder. I was mesmerized, delighted and appreciative, as if it were Christmas morning and I was unwrapping a very expensive gift. He stole my breath when he chose that moment to penetrate me.

I was completely diverted by the sight of him, so wrapped up in my own musings that I didn't feel him move. One moment we were separate, and the next, he slid so completely inside that I gasped in shock. My legs parted automatically, allowing him to settle deep within. He moved his hand from the base of his rod to my hip, then around to my buttocks to ease himself deeper.

Shuddering, I moaned, knowing that I was supposed to remain silent, but unable to comply. He was everything I thought he might be and more. His width stretched my tunnel, hollowing me out and filling me up at the same time. I circled him with my strength, holding him fast as he began to move.

Up and down he glided, washing me out from within, taking hold of my heart and never letting go. I could vaguely sense the couch around us, the expensive leather cushions acting almost like a second skin beneath me. His motions rocked the boat, making my chest bounce and the furniture squeak.

I dragged my fingernails up his arms, cresting at his biceps and his shoulders, diving down past his upper back to meet at his spine. I wanted all of him, every last inch. I wanted to gorge myself on his flesh, to hit the high note and send all my reservations packing. I needed him to complete me, more than I had ever needed a man in my life.

Everything about him was intoxicating. He was so strong and in control. In the office and in the bedroom, his word was law. Everything fell into place the moment he made his wishes known. He pumped into my core, straining and grinding, taking his pleasure as if he was accustomed to it. I longed to push him over the edge, to see the fireworks explode in his eyes.

It was a project I would gladly take on. I wanted that final bit of pleasure, the knowledge that I was the one who brought him to his knees. That was the last thought that passed through my mind before the orgasm took over.

I wanted him to cum. I wanted to gaze into his eyes and watch the transformation. Instead, I gripped him hard and doubled over, drowning in pure delight. He thundered through his final strokes, beating me into the couch as I floated sweetly in my own mind. A moment later, he, too, seized up, his muscles tensing as he released his final load.

I wrapped my arms around him, drawing him down into my embrace. He was hot and a thin film of sweat greased our bodies. I felt his heart racing, having just completed its ultimate objective. His breath came swift and deep with the practiced tempo of an athlete. We lay there together, him on top, me on bottom, for a few minutes.

When he pulled back, he was grinning, and I saw with relief the person that I wanted to unveil. For the moment, he was without reserve. He was completely in the moment, and happy to be there. Gone was all the people pleasing nonsense and the burning desire to be the best. He was just Nate, innocent and free, proud to have spent an hour pleasuring me.

He climbed off me awkwardly and began to hunt for his clothes. I came up off the couch, hearing the protest of the cushions as I removed my weight. We dressed and sat back down to pull on our shoes. Far from being ashamed of what had just happened, I felt closer to him than ever before. We were partners in this deception, equally culpable and equally in danger of consequences if word ever got out.

"Is there anything else I can do for you before I go?" I teased.

He gave me a sideways look, as if he didn't appreciate the joke. "I'll walk you down."

"Really?" I was surprised. I expected him to stay and work late as he always did. Why should one passionate sexual encounter change everything?

"Really. I'm not going to be able to get any work done anyway." That last statement was made sardonically, and I couldn't help but feel disappointed. It looked like we were back to the way things used to be. He was using humor to deflect from true connection. He wasn't ready to admit that anything meaningful had happened.

I was surprised and delighted when he walked me all the way to my car. I hadn't been expecting such royal treatment. Although, objectively, he may have figured it was probably the least he could do after taking advantage of me in his office. I didn't feel that way. Our relationship had nothing to do with our jobs.

During the day, he was CEO and I was a secretary. But after hours, we were two consenting adults. I got just as much satisfaction from our lovemaking as he did, maybe even more. At least I was willing to concede that something important had happened. He seemed to want to bounce right back into our work relationship instead of headstrong lovers. But he was in charge, so I had to follow his lead.

At my car, he pulled me into his arms again. As he kissed me passionately beneath the heavy cement ceiling in the dimly lit alcove of the parking garage, I felt my heart begin to quicken again. This was an added bonus, unexpected because it was out in the open. If he wasn't careful, people would begin to talk.

I didn't fight it, but I couldn't deny the monster of desire springing back to life inside me. I wondered if this was just the beginning of another roll in the hay, but just when the fire started burning, he broke away.

His eyes were haunted as he gazed at me, and I knew he was reliving our adventure upstairs.

"See you tomorrow," he rasped. He reached for his tie, forgetting for a moment that he hadn't put it back on.

I smiled politely, not trusting myself to anything more. I ducked into my front seat, my head spinning. Nate was definitely trouble, although the good, heart lifting, toe curling kind. I wondered what tomorrow would bring, and how often we could get together without anyone else finding out.

All the reasons not to sleep with my boss fled my mind, leaving a single, solitary hope. I wanted him again. Once just wasn't enough. I was willing to risk everything, my job, my future, and my reputation, just to have him inside me a second time. He gave me a taste of paradise, but I was greedy. I didn't need a crystal ball to know that he felt the same way.

Chapter 19

Nate

I watched her drive away, thinking about what I had just done. It wasn't anywhere near the desk, but that didn't help matters. I fell into the same pattern as my father, unable to resist temptation when it was so close to my workspace.

Ava deserved better. She deserved a man who was interested in a happily ever after. I didn't like emotions and I didn't want anything permanent. I was just looking for a good time, and I didn't properly explain that before it began.

When she reached into my pants, I was shocked. But she knew what she was doing. No man on earth could have resisted that. I followed my heart, or rather, my dick, and ended up screwing her on the sofa.

Afterwards, I didn't want it to end, so I kissed her. But then I was afraid she would get the wrong idea. I couldn't back out without seeming like an asshole and I couldn't move forward without making myself uncomfortable.

I wasn't sure what to do, so I walked back up to the fifth floor and knocked on Peter's door. He was still there. Like me, he tended to work early and work late. It was the sign of a dedicated executive and I encouraged it. I couldn't ask people to put in more time than they legally had to, but the culture that my father created and which I perpetuated, said that the farther up the food chain you got, the more time you were expected to put in.

I opened the door when he invited me in and pulled up a chair beside his desk. "You want to go out for drinks?" I asked.

"Sure," he replied, always up for an adventure. "Is everything okay?"

"I'll tell you all about it, but not here," I said.

"Do you want to take one car?"

"Sure," I replied. I could leave my car in the parking garage and have Peter swing back by on our way home.

"Just let me finish this email," he requested.

"I'll go grab my wallet," I said, standing up.

We met in my reception area a few minutes later. I couldn't help glancing at Ava's desk and Peter caught it. "Trouble with the secretary?"

"Let's just get out of the building," I replied. For some reason, it felt like we would get caught if I said anything within these four walls.

Peter drove to our favorite bar. It was an upscale place with expensive drinks and a discerning clientele. The place itself was down to earth though, with warm wooden tables and a fun atmosphere. Boston was one of the oldest cities in the country. It predated the Declaration of Independence by a few hundred years. I didn't know how old the bar was, but I knew that it passed its centennial.

"So, what's going on? I'm dying to know," Peter said as we slid into a booth.

"I fucked Ava," I announced.

Far from the office, I felt more comfortable revealing my secret. It had only been a few minutes, maybe an hour, since the deed went down. I could still feel her body beneath mine. The sensual way she squirmed under my attention was distracting. I wanted more of it, but I didn't want to break her heart.

"You dog!" Peter cried, louder than I wanted him to.

"The problem is, what if she thinks this is the start of a relationship?"

"Why are you shooting yourself in the foot before you even get started?" Peter complained. "Let yourself enjoy it."

"What happens when it all falls apart? How am I going to work with her then?"

"Maybe it won't fall apart." He played with his napkin, folding it in half and then unfolding it. "Maybe you'll fall in love."

I gave him a stern gaze, telling him that I wasn't interested in playing games. "This is me we're talking about."

"So, add her name to your list of willing accomplices," Peter teased.

"That's just the problem," I explained. "I don't think she wants her name added to that list."

"I see." Peter stroked his chin. "Well, you can't bring up your other girlfriends—"

"I don't have any girlfriends."

"Other friends?"

"Okay," I allowed.

"You can't bring up your other friends if you think she wants exclusivity."

"Exactly."

"It's a tough spot," he mused.

I thought about Ava. It seemed like she was the only thing on my mind. What was it about her and her quiet determination? She was all prim and proper during the day, but she turned into an animal as soon as I made a move.

I wasn't thinking correctly. I was letting my body lead the way instead of my mind. I needed to have a conversation with her, to explain what I was looking for, and what I was not looking for. It would be a kindness. We needed to get on the same page or we couldn't let what happened before happen again.

That talk was not going to go well. I could just imagine her face falling, her little heart breaking at the news. I felt like a monster. Why had I let myself get carried away? Why had I even kissed her to begin with? I tried to remember the first genuine interaction we had. It was in the parking garage after our meeting with Jonas. That was my downfall. I didn't want to see her in the arms of another man. But if I wanted her all to myself, didn't it follow that I should offer her the same concession?

I decided to sleep on it. Until I brought the subject up, all options were on the table. I would only be married to a certain course of action once I took that first step. I relaxed, allowing myself to enjoy the drinks and the atmosphere.

Peter and I began to talk about different things and we ended the evening on a high note. I went home fully satisfied in a way I hadn't experienced since taking over the family business. Whether that was about Ava or about my father, I wasn't sure. All I knew was that things were settled in my heart and my abdomen. There was no nervous energy, no fire that needed to be put out.

I went to bed content with the way things were working out. If my dreams were all about Ava, so what? That didn't mean I was falling for the woman. I just had a delightful time with her in the office, and I was going to let fate decide what was in store. I didn't have to commit to anything I didn't want to. In the meantime, I would control my libido as much as I could, although if I tripped up again, who stood to get hurt? Ava was a grown up as was I. She had more than proved that she could take care of herself.

Chapter 20

Ava

I wasn't a fool. I knew that one sexual encounter didn't mean Nate and I were going steady. There was plenty of room for experimentation and I wasn't expecting a marriage proposal. However, that final kiss in the parking garage gave me hope that there might be more in store for us later in the week.

I came into the office the next day, prepared to act as if nothing happened. We had to be very careful about showing affection around other people. Not only that, but I knew I had to be careful about showing affection around Nate.

This wasn't my first rodeo; I knew that most men wanted something casual. That didn't mean that a more serious arrangement was off the table. It just meant that I couldn't start picking out China patterns yet. If he thought I was going to go all misty eyed and follow him around everywhere, he was mistaken. Sex was just that, sex. I wanted more of it, but I didn't want Nate to feel trapped.

I was independent enough to relax and let the roll of the dice point me in the right direction.

I was surprised to see a bouquet of flowers on my desk. If Nate wanted to keep our tryst a secret, he was doing a very poor job. How was I going to explain flowers from my boss? I hurried to my desk, thinking that I needed to hide them. Everyone who came through the reception area would see them, and they would know exactly what we had been up to.

I almost didn't read the card. I was so convinced that Nate sent them. I didn't even think that he was the send flowers kind of guy. He was gruff and efficient, even if I knew he had a heart of gold. Flowers seemed a bit over the top, maybe even possessive. It was a signal to the rest of the staff, loud and clear, that I was taken.

I plucked the card off its little plastic fork and nearly had a heart attack. They weren't from Nate at all, but from Marcus. How did he know where I worked? I thought I had solved that problem by shutting off my phone. If he tracked me down, how did he do it? Was he driving around the city searching for me? Was there a GPS tracking device on my old phone that was still working? Did he have friends who were working for him? Maybe he hired a private detective.

All those thoughts raced through my head as I stood, nailed to the spot. I couldn't breathe. I felt my airways collapsing. My heart thundered in my ears. This was the worst possible thing that could happen. Marcus invaded my space. He invaded my new life with his evil and vindictive personality.

I didn't understand why he was sending me flowers. He was the one who kicked me out. He didn't give a crap about me the whole time I was homeless, allowing me to eat out of a soup kitchen and sleep in the backseat of my car. Yet as soon as I found a job and was starting to put my life back together, he decided he wanted me back.

I re-read the missive on the note. It said: *I miss you. Marcus.*

He missed me? What the heck was that all about? It couldn't be true. He had that other woman to entertain him. He didn't need me. Didn't he know how intrusive this gift would be? I already blocked him and then turned off my phone. Couldn't he take the hint?

I picked up the vase, intending to throw it in the trash. My hands were shaking and I dropped it. Water and glass exploded onto the floor, a wave of liquid carrying shards halfway across the room.

I screamed in frustration. I would have to clean it up quickly before anyone could see. I was down on my hands and knees, picking up flower petals when Nate opened his door. I looked up, unable to contain my alarm. He read my face and crouched beside me, concerned.

"What happened?"

"These are from Marcus," I said. Even the words sounded like a betrayal. I had such a nice time with Nate the previous night and it seemed like Marcus just wanted to ruin that. Maybe he had. Maybe that was the point of the flowers. But if that was the case, it was even worse than I suspected. That would mean that Marcus knew all about Nate, and that was a level of intrusion that I didn't want to contemplate.

"I'll get someone to clean it up," Nate said, helping me to my feet.

"He knows where I work," I told my boss. I wanted to explain the rationale behind breaking the vase. It wasn't just unwanted roses; it was the implicit knowledge that came with his gift. He wanted to tell me that he knew where I worked. That was terrifying and so much worse than any insult or injury.

"I'll let security know," Nate assured me.

"How did he find out?" I wondered out loud. It wouldn't help me to have security on the lookout if Marcus was stalking me from across the street. I wondered if he was tracking my car, or if he had talked to any of my friends. Not knowing where he got his information made it difficult to remain calm.

Nate read it all and took me by the hand, pulling me close. "You're safe."

"I don't feel safe," I mumbled.

"Try not to think about it," he said.

The shock threw me off balance and I had a hard time recovering enough to focus on my work. Nate had someone come by to clean up the mess. I sat at my desk, watching him mop. I tried not to make eye contact, but I couldn't help watching.

The janitor scraped the remaining stems into the trash and swept the broken glass into a dustpan. He toweled the floor off and then wiped it clean, emptying my trash can into a larger one on wheels.

When he left, there was very little evidence. A small part of the floor was wet, but that dried soon enough. I knew that the janitor was wondering what had happened. If he thought that Nate and I had been in a fight or that someone had thrown the vase, he didn't say. I wasn't going to tell my whole sordid story anyway, so it didn't really matter. I hoped it wouldn't get back to me in the form of gossip. I had more important things to worry about at the moment.

I couldn't keep my eyes off the window. Every time a car drove past, I jumped. We were on the fifth floor, so there wasn't a lot of noise that reached us. But there was some and it was too much.

Nate found me staring at the computer screen, my eyes full of unshed tears. It was nearing lunch time and I knew he had an appointment soon. I had to get myself together if I was going to welcome his guests.

He took one look at me and sighed. "You should go home."

"I'm fine," I said stubbornly, wiping my eyes.

Any makeup I put on that morning was probably smudged by then. I couldn't see myself but I knew that he could. He was being patient, but also needed a functioning secretary. I was less professional than I should have been and it was all Marcus's fault.

"Ava, I'll be fine," Nate soothed, helping me to my feet. "I'll get Peter's secretary to sit here."

I didn't want to be replaceable. I wanted to do my job and be good at it. That was the high horse I was riding on when Marcus kicked me off. I didn't have a choice though. I wasn't competent to remain in the office. I would have to go back home and shake it off. Maybe I could do some boxing, or some other cardio that would help relieve the nervous tension.

I was just afraid that once I stepped foot outside the building, Marcus would swoop in. Not knowing where he was or how he got his intel was torture. I consoled myself with the knowledge that the place I was staying was built to shield women from jealous lovers. There was an entire nonprofit helping me hide from him, even though I had been unaware at the beginning that I needed to keep my location secret.

Nodding, I inhaled bravely, determined to retain as much of my dignity as possible. At least it was only Nate seeing me this way. If it was the rest of the office, if I had to work in a cubicle among the finance department or the salespeople, I would have been mortified. Whatever sick and twisted game Marcus was playing, he had the upper hand. I needed to gather my resources, maybe reach out to Mariah to let her know what was happening.

That was the best plan I had come up with so far. Of course, Mariah would know what to do. She helped dozens, maybe even hundreds, of women get out from under abusive boyfriends. She would know how to help me.

"Okay," I answered Nate. "I'll go. Thank you."

"Take the day, and if you still feel bad tomorrow, give me a call."

"I might call your mother," I told him. I didn't want Mariah to drop a bomb on him, telling him about our conversation before I could.

"That's a good idea," he approved.

I gathered up my purse and straightened my spine. I would hold my head up high as I walked through the lobby. Nate had security meet me at the front desk. I was about to walk past and go straight to my car when our day guard, Paul, caught up with me.

"Ma'am," he said politely.

"Hello."

"I'm supposed to walk you to your vehicle," Paul explained.

I didn't reply, though I felt better with an escort. Climbing into the driver's seat, I gave the security guard a little wave. I was out of his hands now and on my own. I felt very small, jumping at shadows. It was a long drive full of heart stopping near misses. But I felt safe when I finally pulled up to my building.

Chapter 21

Nate

I knew Ava couldn't do her job, not the way she was acting that morning. It wasn't that I needed a secretary more than I needed her to be safe, just that I thought by sending her home, I was helping. I figured she could blow off some steam, or maybe curl up with a good book. Whatever she needed to do to make herself feel better obviously couldn't be accomplished in the office.

I called Peter and asked him to loan me his secretary. The other woman poked into my office, curious more than anything. I told her that Ava had come down with something and had to go home. I had a few meetings lined up and asked if she could sit outside and answer phones.

She agreed, getting comfortable in Ava's spot. Only an hour passed before Ava was back, however, breaking into my first meeting. I was on a video call with a colleague on the west coast. We were discussing one of the major distributors, and how much of a pain in the ass they were.

"They think because they've cornered the market, they can just push us around," the man complained.

"What are we going to do?" I asked. "Our hands are tied."

"I have half a mind to tell them to shove it," my friend said. "We can do our own online sales. We can go to their competitor."

The competitor was so far down on the food chain, it wasn't even funny. The distributor we were having a problem with had such a market share, it was ridiculous. I opened my mouth to offer another unhelpful quip when my door opened, and Ava stumbled through.

I could see instantly that something was wrong. "I have to go," I told my colleague.

"Is everything okay?"

"Yeah, I'll call you back," I answered, getting him off the screen. I closed my laptop and ran to her side, helping her onto the couch.

She looked up at me, breathing heavily. She looked like she had just run a marathon in freezing cold weather. Her face was pale, her eyes wide and frightened. I didn't understand what had just happened, where she had been, or why she returned. I fought the urge to berate her, to try to coax the words from her traumatized throat. She would tell me when she could.

"Marcus," she whispered, clutching my hand in desperation. "He left flowers at my door."

"I saw," I replied. I thought we had been over this. The flowers were cleaned up and the situation had resolved itself.

"No." Ava shook her head. "At my apartment."

"But that's supposed to be a secret," I said, dumbfounded.

"I know!" she snapped. "I don't know how he found me. I don't know what to do. Where can I go? Why is he doing this?"

I sat down beside her, feeling like there was a lot I was missing. If this man was the one to end the relationship, why was he stalking her? Surely, he understood that it was inappropriate for him to leave flowers outside her door. The point of the exercise must have been to elicit this type of response. But why would anyone want to frighten someone they cared about?

I was confused, but more than that, I was pissed. "Wait here," I told Ava, getting up and walking to my door. I poked my head outside, politely excusing myself for the rest of the day. I told Peter's secretary to let my calls go to voice mail. I asked her to cancel my remaining meetings and let everyone know I was taking a sick day.

Once the woman returned to her own desk on the opposite side of the hall, I helped Ava to her feet. We walked back down to the parking garage, but instead of putting her in her own car, I took her to mine.

"Where are we going?" she asked.

"I'm going to take you home and you're going to pack a bag," I said determinedly.

"And then?"

"And then I'm taking you to my place," I replied.

She pressed her lips together, considering my request. I knew she wanted to refuse. I knew she didn't want to ask for help, or to be a burden to anyone. Back when her biggest problem was homelessness, she had been downright rude in refusing assistance. But that was child's play compared to what was currently happening.

The whole time she was sleeping outside, she never attracted the kind of attention her ex-boyfriend had literally brought to her doorstep. It had become personal. She wasn't just a number, just an invisible byproduct of the expensive Boston society. She was a victim, or she would be if we couldn't find a way to deflect the boyfriend's unwanted attention. I couldn't bring myself to imagine what might happen if he showed up when she was home all alone. I wasn't going to let that happen.

"I want to say no," Ava began, "but I won't. Thank you."

"Good," I agreed. "I'm glad you see the logic."

"I'm sorry I had to drag you into this."

"You didn't drag me into anything," I assured her. "Marcus did. He's the one who's creating all the drama."

Ava sighed. I could see the relief on her face and knew I was doing the right thing. We drove to her place. It didn't escape me that even though it was supposed to be a secret place known only to the employees of the nonprofit, that I knew where it was. I knew because of my mother's involvement. But if one extra person was aware, it stood to reason that there could be more.

How he found her probably wasn't as important as the fact that he had accomplished it. She was no longer safe in the little hiding spot, so we had to get her out of there. I parked and came up with her. I noticed she threw the flowers away, just as she had tried to at the office. This time, she managed to neatly tuck the entire vase in the trash can, but it was all still there.

Knowing a little bit about flowers (I sent them to my mom every year for her birthday and for Mother's Day), I could see they were expensive. It wasn't a small bouquet, but a medium-sized one, complete with baby's breath and decorative ferns. Whoever Marcus was, he dropped a pretty penny on his threatening message. I guessed that he had some resources at his disposal. It made sense. He was able to uncover her place of residence as well as her place of business.

Ava went straight for the bedroom and pulled a suitcase out of the closet. She loaded it up with a few of the fashions that my mother had given her. She ducked into the bathroom and returned with a well-worn toiletries bag. The speed at which she accomplished all that was astonishing. I was expecting to wait around for at least fifteen to twenty minutes, but she was ready in three.

"I've never seen someone pack so fast," I observed.

She gave me a cold stare, and I realized that I missed her sense of humor. She called me out without a second thought, putting me in my place with just an upturned eyebrow. "You mean you've never seen a woman pack so fast."

"I might mean that," I hesitated, not sure how much I could admit without getting myself in trouble.

"Hmm," she replied, one hand on her hip. "Not all women are high maintenance."

"Not all women have experience being homeless either," I pointed out.

She sighed. "You hit the nail on the head."

"Okay," I agreed. There was no point in standing around arguing. If she was ready, we could just go.

I grabbed the suitcase, against her protests, and walked it out to the car. She followed silently, and I felt as if we were escaping from some overbearing parental figure, or an intrusive governmental agency. It was like the CIA was watching us and we had to be careful. I didn't know how far Marcus's reach extended, and whether he was watching at that exact moment.

Odds were that he had just learned of her whereabouts and sent the flowers to unsettle her. It didn't mean he was hiding out in an apartment across the street with a pair of binoculars. But it didn't mean he *wasn't* hiding out across the street, I told myself. I had to be prepared for anything, even hand to hand combat if it came down to that. Hopefully the guy didn't have a gun.

I hustled Ava into my car and sped off. My own home was in a gated community, so there was a little bit more protection afforded there. We parked and I walked around to open the door for her.

I could see she was recovering from her shock somewhat. Escorting her inside, I put her suitcase down near the door. There were two extra rooms I had for guests, one with a queen-sized bed and one with two twins. I walked her to the room with one bed, turning on the lights so she could have a look around.

This guest room came with its own bathroom. I showed her the shower and suggested she might want to make use of it. She declined.

"I'm not really in a mood to be naked," she said.

"That's a pity," I replied, the words out before I realized how vulgar they sounded. "I'm going to go make us something to eat."

"I'd like to call your mom, if that's okay," she asked.

"Of course."

I don't know why I didn't think of it sooner. Mom was exactly the person to help us understand this conundrum. She had experience with victims of domestic violence before. She had connections in the community who helped women restart their lives after stalking and harassment. If she couldn't do anything for us, at least she would know who to call.

I went into the kitchen to work on a meal while Ava got in touch with my mom. I wanted to go straight to the gym and punch out some of my frustrations, but I also wanted to remain accessible. If I was busy beating the bag to death, Ava might not want to interrupt me. She might see me doing it and be turned off, or she might worry about my own headspace.

Cooking was almost as soothing as working out. I decided to make something that was healthy but had a bunch of steps. That way I could zone out and get into the rhythm, picking myself up so that I could be a better support for Ava. I settled on grilled chicken with peppers and zucchini.

I cut onions first, then sliced the peppers lengthwise before stirring them together. A little bit of olive oil brought out the flavors, and as the vegetables cooked, I considered what the rest of the day was going to look like.

Reflecting, I realized I couldn't help feeling protective of Ava. Our single exchange didn't mean that I was her boyfriend, but it gave me some stake in the outcome. Certainly, Marcus would be interested to know that we were intimate, if he didn't know it already. Maybe that's what prompted this renewed interest in Ava as a life partner. Maybe he found out somehow that she was moving on and decided not to let her.

I should be mad. I should be furious at the guy for messing with her. Instead, I felt numb. I got through thirty-three years without dealing with this kind of crap. I had countless interactions with women, but none of them had been stalked. At least not to my knowledge. Maybe it was because I never cared enough to find out. Maybe some of my other hook ups were dealing with things they would rather not talk about.

The thought made me sick. It was painful to be a part of the same gender as some guy who tried to intimidate women that way. I wanted to apologize to Ava on behalf of all men, but I knew that wouldn't help. I was thrilled when the doorbell rang, knowing it was probably my mom. I turned the burner down and went to answer it, welcoming her into my home.

"Ava's in the guest room," I said.

Mom walked down the hall, knocking on Ava's door. I turned back to my cooking. By the time I had the meal plated and on the table, Ava and my mother emerged from the guest room. Ava looked a lot more composed than she had before. She wasn't crying and her shoulders were straight.

Her hair was down, and it framed her face in a way I didn't usually get to see. I remembered our erotic play in the office and how her body looked stretched out beneath mine. I knew the curve of her breasts and the slope of her backside.

I shook my head. It was not the time for such thoughts. She was vulnerable and shaken. I needed to be supportive, not seductive. The two women sat down to eat, and I joined them. There was no space for small talk, and neither of them were comfortable enough with the subject to discuss it in front of me.

It was an awkward meal, and when we were done, I stood up quickly. "You guys can go continue your conversation. I'll clean up."

They followed my suggestion without complaint, walking out to the porch. I watched them through the window, my mother and my…? What was Ava to me? She was obviously my secretary, but I felt like there was something more.

We weren't boyfriend and girlfriend; we weren't husband and wife. And yet, there was some possessive component to what I was doing for her. I didn't want anyone to mess with her because it made her scared and sad, but also because I thought of her as *mine*. No one should mess with something or someone that belonged to me. If that bastard came around again, I would make him pay.

Chapter 22

Ava

Talking with Mariah calmed me down. Just as I suspected, she knew all about abusive exes. She gave me advice and listened as I spoke. We wound our way through my entire relationship, right up to the end.

"It is strange that he's become so possessive months after the end of the relationship," Mariah said.

"It totally blindsided me," I agreed. "I mean, where was all this affection when we were dating? He didn't love me."

"He still doesn't," Nate's mom said. "It's more about power and dominance than it is about love. He used to have you in his life to control, and now he doesn't. He's missing that piece."

I frowned, unable to fit the entire puzzle together.

"When you were together, did he tell you how to do things? How to wash the dishes or how to dress, that type of thing?"

"All the time," I exclaimed. "I could never do anything right. I thought that's why he started cheating on me, because I didn't live up to his standards."

"Mm-hmm," she murmured. "I've seen it before. For him, it is less about the specific things he wants you to do, although he might think that's what it was about. But he really just wants to control you."

I lowered my head down to my chest in exhaustion. Even talking about Marcus was draining. I wished that he would just go away and leave me alone. He had his chance, and he ruined it for both of us.

"There was a time when I would have been excited to receive flowers from him," I admitted.

"Of course," Mariah said. "These abusers are often very charming in the beginning."

I was having a hard time thinking of Marcus as an abuser. Even after his unwanted texts and unwanted flowers, I didn't want to consider myself a battered woman. He never hit me, so I suppose technically I wasn't abused. That was a comforting thought, but one I didn't share. Mariah seemed so sure of herself and her knowledge of my situation. I didn't want to interrupt her wisdom with facts.

Suddenly, I thought about my own mother and wished that I could be with her instead. It wasn't that Mariah was unhelpful. She was enormously helpful. She was the one person who was kind enough and experienced enough to show me the way. But she was so different from my own mom, and that just made me miss my family more.

I grew up in a small town in Virginia, and my parents expected me to go to community college and take a job as a dental assistant or a secretary in the elementary school. Mom was forever showing me "ladylike" career paths that might lead to a husband and children down the road. She was appalled when I decided to pursue journalism. To her mind, it wasn't an appropriate calling for a single young woman.

I stood my ground, applying to college in Boston. When I was accepted, she basically disowned me. She threw me out and told me not to come back. It began what had apparently turned into a tradition. Although back then, I was able to move into the dorms, and I wasn't actually homeless.

Still, it hurt. Even after all these years, my mother stuck to her guns. She didn't contact me and I didn't contact her. Talking to Mariah just made that wound a little more obvious. I wished for what Nate had: enough money never to worry about sleeping in his car, and a family that cared about him. Even his father, though I understood there was some bad blood there, cared enough to come around and try to talk to his son.

I didn't want to dwell. Explaining my situation would only have made it more painful. I stuck to the current dilemma and allowed Mariah to think all my tears were just because of Marcus.

"Are you staying the night here?" I asked her. The sun was starting to lower, turning the horizon orange and red.

"No, sweetheart," Mariah said, standing up. "In fact, I have to go. You'll be safe with Nate."

"But for how long?" I wondered.

"Don't worry about it," Mariah replied. "We'll send someone around to collect all of your things, and we can move you to a different apartment."

"What if he finds me there?" I demanded. I wasn't sure if I was ever going to feel safe on my own again. If Marcus could find me in one hideout, he could find the next. I was sure of it.

"One thing at a time," Mariah counseled.

I took a deep breath. She was right, of course. I couldn't obsess over the next insult when it hadn't even happened yet. I would bunk with Nate for the night, and allow Mariah's organization to help me in the morning.

"If there's anything else you need…" Mariah said before leaving.

"I can't ask you for anything else," I demurred. "You both have given me too much already."

"Nonsense," Mariah scoffed, pressing her lips to my forehead. She stood up, every bit the mother in the situation. "We're billionaires. We can afford to help out a friend."

I stood up along with her, ready to go back inside. I wasn't comfortable sitting on the porch by myself. It was some crazy notion that Marcus might be driving by at any moment. Although, with the gate and the guard, that was unlikely.

It was easy to forget that Nate was a billionaire. Obviously, I knew he was CEO of a multinational company. He was accustomed to getting his way even though once I got to know him, I could see he had a soft side. I wondered if he had a yacht, or if he had property in other parts of the world.

Compared with what he likely had, putting me up for a night was negligible. We could just go to work together tomorrow. Not a big deal. I felt better, though I still didn't want to become a burden. It was all fun and games now, but what if I needed more long-term assistance? I resolved not to accept a penny more than I had to.

Walking back inside, I couldn't find Nate. I walked from room to room, searching for him, and got a self-guided tour of his home. I didn't want to go upstairs. Whatever was up there was probably personal. I stuck to the lower level, but even so, it seemed like there were dozens of rooms.

I finally found him all the way in the back, in a room that had been turned into a home gym. There was a treadmill and a rack of weights, but Nate wasn't focused on either of those things. He was standing in the middle of the space, shirtless, punching a device that looked like the offspring of a robot and a boxing bag.

I didn't want to disturb him, so I turned away. But he must have heard me in the doorway because he stopped and turned around. "Did my mother leave?" he asked.

"Yes," I said.

His shoulders relaxed as he reached for his wrist, peeling the gloves off one by one.

"You don't have to stop," I insisted.

"I was just letting off steam."

"I'm sorry for all this drama," I told him.

"It's not your fault."

"I feel like it's a little bit my fault," I argued.

He gave me a look, turning my insides to jelly. I knew it wasn't the right time for affection, but he made it hard to walk away. We went into the living room together, and Nate poured us each a glass of wine. I didn't want to get drunk, but figured that a single glass was okay.

"I'm sorry I interrupted your day," I began.

"Don't worry about it," he said.

I didn't know if we should talk about what happened in the office. It hadn't been very long and our ardor hadn't cooled at all, judging from the barely contained sexual tension that was zinging through the room. I decided not to bring it up. It was better left undisturbed, bubbling just below the surface. It wasn't the right time to act on it, but who knew what the next day would bring?

I excused myself after finishing my glass. I wanted to let him get back to whatever it was he was doing. If I couldn't offer release through sex, then at least I could make myself scarce. I went back to the guest room to grab my toiletries bag.

I really didn't want to be naked, but I knew I couldn't inhabit Nate's space without taking a shower. As a respectful guest, it only made sense to keep myself clean. I could wash away all the anxiety and the stress sweat that I had been sitting in for the past few hours.

Knowing that I was safe, and that Marcus couldn't touch me, I closed the bathroom door and turned on the faucet. I had my own shampoo and a little bottle of body wash. Taking my clothes off, I stepped into the spray, determined to accomplish my objective as quickly as possible.

I wondered what Nate was doing. Had he gone back to the gym to work out? Did he stay in the living room and turn on the television? Maybe he went upstairs to his own room in order to decompress.

I finished my shower without incident, toweling off and getting dressed. It was still a little early, but I was exhausted and wanted to sleep.

My thoughts were scattered; I felt like I was living a nightmare. Maybe if I went to sleep things would be better the next day. I threw in the towel, not even cluing Nate into my plans. It was best all around if I ended the day and tried again in the morning.

I opted to sleep in my clothes instead of pajamas. The time at the homeless shelter taught me that letting down my guard was dangerous. By wearing sweatpants instead of pajama bottoms, I would be prepared for the unexpected.

I paired the sweatpants with a T-shirt and a sweatshirt, everything I needed to roll out of bed and fight off an intruder. Pulling the covers up to my chin, I tried to shut off my brain. The day's events were playing through my mind, taunting me with echoes of my former life.

I wished that Marcus would just go back where he came from. I was almost over him and then he forced himself back in. I knew he did it deliberately. His flowers were having their desired effect, making me think about him and worry about where he was. He wanted me to know that I wasn't safe anywhere. He wanted to prove that he could have me again any time he wanted me.

It was a blatant lie, and I had to remind myself of that. I was my own person. I didn't belong to him anymore than I belonged to my parents. I was independent and adventurous. I had survived living on the streets. I made some good friends who were going to help me land on my feet, and I needed to focus on the future going forward.

With determination, I managed to turn my thoughts away from Marcus. I tried counting sheep and drifted off finally to visions of fluffy white animals hopping a fence. It was early when I woke up, but I knew I had to go to work. Nate wouldn't want to take another day off, and I felt strong enough to do my job.

I met him at the breakfast table, already dressed and ready to go. He was the utmost professional, eliminating any hint of the sexual tension that had been ripe the night before. He wore a suit and tie without the jacket. On the table was a breakfast to rival even the most expensive hotels.

There were fresh oranges, crispy bacon, and scrambled eggs. There were croissants and jelly and strong coffee. I poured myself a cup and sat down, reaching for a stick of bacon.

"You really like to cook?" I asked, impressed.

"It calms me down."

"You need to calm down?"

"What's the game plan?" he turned the spotlight back to me.

"Your mother said she'll have someone pick up my stuff and move me into a different apartment."

"And how do you feel about that?" He studied my face, looking for signs of honesty.

I knew I had to tell him the truth, no matter what that meant. "I'm a little nervous."

He nodded. Apparently, he wasn't surprised. Thinking about it logically, I couldn't see why anyone wouldn't be nervous. I only had one night free from worry, and I was going to have to go back to living alone.

Marcus was nothing if not resourceful. I was sure he would find me again, and when he did, I wasn't going to run to Nate for protection. I could see it all as if it had already happened. I kept my mouth shut. What was important was going back to work and being the best secretary I could be. I didn't want to rely on Nate and his family, no matter how rich and well connected they were. I didn't care if helping me was easy for them.

We finished up our meal and got into the car. Driving to work felt almost domestic. We were like a legitimate couple, leaving our home and carpooling to the office. I felt relaxed as we walked in together. Nate had no need to use his badge, and since I was with him, the guard didn't ask for mine either.

It was the start of a new day. There were new possibilities and a ton of work to do. All the meetings that Nate canceled the day before had to be rescheduled. There was the new line to approve and a dozen new distributors to contact. It was a busy day, and I was looking forward to sinking my teeth into it. Things were only going to get better; I could feel it.

Chapter 23

Nate

I had two agendas when I got to the office. The first was to try to convince Ava to file a police report. She didn't seem to understand the trouble she was in. She kept deflecting my concern, telling me that Marcus wasn't really dangerous. I wasn't fooled. I distinctly recalled the look on her face when she stumbled into my office the day before. She had been terrified.

Having a night free from worry had done wonders. She was back on her feet and as effective as ever. She arranged all my meetings and made sure that I got all the preliminary information in time to digest it. But I wasn't looking for a super secretary at the moment.

I wanted Ava to be safe, and I thought the best way to go about it was to get the authorities involved. I called my mother to see if I could get someone else on my side. If Ava wouldn't listen to me, it was possible she would take direction from Mariah.

"Good morning," I said into the speakerphone.

It was around eleven in the morning, and I had just concluded the first of many meetings. Ava was outside in the reception area, hard at work. I was hoping I could get my mom on board and then call Ava into the conversation. We could double time her, getting her to file that report despite her objections. I knew that Marcus was dangerous, and that by just alerting the police to the problem, she would be in a better position. If he decided to show up at her doorstep, she would have more ammunition.

"Good morning, sweetheart," Mom said. "How did you sleep?"

"Fine."

"How is Ava?"

"That's what I wanted to talk to you about." I drew a breath before continuing, ready to argue my case. "I want her to file a police report, but she says that her ex isn't that dangerous and she doesn't want to 'bother' the police."

"That bit about not bothering the police is ridiculous," my mother scoffed. "But I understand her reluctance to make the conflict official."

"I don't," I snapped. "What if he comes back? What if he shows up at the office? She should at least put it on record that he's harassing her."

"I agree," Mom responded hesitantly.

"But?" I could sense there was more to her reaction than she was saying.

"But it's really not up to us, is it?" Mom concluded.

I rolled my eyes. I didn't see why it wasn't up to me. Surely my feelings for Ava bought me some consideration. I was just as much a part of her life as the ex was. And that realization brought me to the second item on my agenda.

I wanted Ava to stay with me. I didn't want to push her out into some other tiny crappy apartment. I didn't like emotions and hadn't ever felt attached to a woman before, but Ava was different. There was something about her poise and her strength of character that turned me on. Remembering how forward she had been with me in my office, I almost grew hard sitting at my desk.

I wasn't going to let her walk away, unless she was the one who pushed me. Circumstances be damned, I wanted her in my home, in my bed if at all possible. The night before, drinking wine with her in the living room had been torture. Neither of us let ourselves do what we both wanted to do. No one made the first move, and it remained awkward until Ava cut it short.

Hearing her take a shower, I fought the urge to barge into the bathroom. I knew I couldn't take advantage of her in her time of need, but damn it was hard. With another twenty-four hours between us and the crisis, I thought this night might be different. If I could convince her to come home with me again and forget about the charity apartment for the moment, I could have my way with her.

I thought about all the things we could do in my home, in my bed, and nearly salivated over the prospect. There had to be a way to offer my house on a more permanent basis. It wasn't that I wanted to marry the woman, but a few more nights would be welcome. The fact that I had never felt that way about anyone else in my life didn't escape me. I had to be cautious. Too much and I risked scaring myself away, too little and I would end up feeling deprived. There had to be a happy medium, and I was convinced it started with Ava spending the weekend.

"You said you were going to find her another place," I told my mother.

"Yes," she agreed. "There are a few more apartments we have available."

"Why don't you have your people deliver her stuff to my place?" I asked. "You can take your time getting the next apartment ready for her."

"The next apartment is already ready," Mom said without missing a beat, "but leave it up to Ava. Whatever she wants to do is fine by me."

"Thanks, Mom," I said, hanging up the phone. I wasn't going to get anything over on her. I knew she liked Ava, and the possibility of seeing her around in the future was too good for a mother to pass up.

I had to approach Ava with the idea, but waited until the last minute. She came into my office around three, a little frustrated.

"I can't get a hold of your mother," she complained. "I don't know where I'm going to sleep tonight."

"You can sleep with me," I said abruptly, getting out of my chair and crossing the room.

Ava stood there in her purple knee-length dress, her eyes wide, watching me. She worried her hands in front of her, obviously taken aback by my bluntness. I wanted to make the offer seem unimportant, like I had an extra room, why wouldn't she use it? But the truth of the matter was that I wasn't offering her the guest room.

A slow smile spread across her face as she absorbed the invitation. "I don't—"

I snaked one hand behind her back, pulling her close. "I don't want to scare you."

"You don't scare me."

"Then forget about the next apartment, and come home with me tonight," I whispered.

"Okay," she replied, tilting her head up for a kiss.

I didn't leave her hanging. Touching my lips to hers, I reclaimed my place in her life. I might not be a boyfriend, but I was something. We had a connection, and it was delicious. I wanted to fuck her right there in the office, but I restrained myself. It was growing late, and I would have to take her home soon. We could wait until we arrived at my place.

I didn't want to be that horn dog who can't keep his hands off his secretary. But even though I fought to avoid the negative connotations, I couldn't wait to see her naked. I surprised myself with the strength of my convictions, and yet it all felt right. Ava and I were meant for each other.

Chapter 24

Ava

The next few hours were torture. I had to resume my spot outside Nate's door, my head full of images of him naked. I knew exactly how he looked. I remembered walking in on him the night before, topless, working the bag. He was beautiful and protective, and he cared about me. It was an intoxicating trifecta that stoked my fire and made my skin tight and uncomfortable.

I longed to run my fingers down his chest, to feel the wealth of muscle beneath his clothing. And I wanted him to touch me too, to resume his patient attention to my breasts and my shoulders.

I wasn't even concerned about what he might think of my birthmark. Unlike other men, including Marcus, who made me feel self-conscious, Nate made light of it with a kiss. I couldn't wait to fall into his arms.

Maybe we would take a bath together, or we could just go straight to his bed. I half expected him to bend me over the desk and dirty up the office once again, but he restrained himself.

It was beginning to be a habit between us, denying our passionate urges. It was never the right time or the right place. We were continuously having to shelve our animal instincts because of other people. I was tired of it.

I almost walked back into his office to demand his attention. I was sure that if I climbed into his lap, he would be unable to resist. But I made myself hold off, knowing that it was better all around if we waited. We would have all night to explore each other's bodies; I didn't need to do it right away.

As soon as the work day was over, however, I was eager to get started. Nate must have felt the same way, because he closed his office at five on the dot. Holding his briefcase, he waited while I put on the away messages. If anyone wanted to get ahold of him between now and the following morning, they were just going to have to wait.

It took me a few seconds, and Nate stood impatiently, glancing at his watch. Instead of sitting, I was leaning over my desk to type on the computer. I felt a hand grazing my backside and looked up to see Nate innocently turn away.

I grinned. It was going to be like that, was it? I straightened, reaching for my purse. "I'm ready."

He walked me to the elevator, and we rode down in silence. I glanced over at him, my entire body aching to wrap itself around his. I could hit the emergency button to stop the ride and undo the tie from around his neck. We could relieve the pressure right there in the elevator. I knew he wanted to. Yet he studied the corner of the box, ignoring me completely.

I wasn't fooled. I could see the tension running through him. Every breath was shallow, every blink of his eye disguising his lust. When the elevator doors opened onto the parking garage, he walked out, pretending not to notice me. I followed assertively, just a fellow co-worker going to the same car.

He clicked the doors open and got into the driver's seat. I walked around to the passenger seat and climbed inside. We closed the doors and looked at each other finally. He was grinning so wide; I thought the smile would break through his cheeks. Without waiting any longer, he reached across the divide, pulling me close.

Our lips met and the space between us dissolved. We became one, the beating of our hearts synchronized, the heat of our tongues intertwined. I lost myself in the kiss. The hard plastic of the parking brake faded away, replaced by the soft insistence of his hand.

I wanted to climb over the obstacles between us and come to rest in his lap. I wanted to take his head in both hands and feel the softness of his close-cropped hair. I wanted to loosen the tie around his neck, undo the buttons on his shirt and reveal his handsome chest. But we were still in the parking garage. If anybody wanted to leave at that exact moment, they would see Mr. Brockman with his secretary making out in his car.

I pulled back. "Drive," I rasped, desperate to get somewhere safe.

I didn't have to tell him twice. "Buckle up."

I pulled at the seat belt, clicking it into place. We sped away, leaving the office in the rear-view mirror. It took about fifteen minutes to reach Nate's neighborhood. We drove through the gate and up to his driveway. Getting out of the car, I held myself in check. To all appearances, we were just an average couple, walking up to our front porch after a long day at work.

But as soon as the door closed behind us, and we were safe from prying eyes, all bets were off. I wrapped my arms around him, eager to bring him as close as physically possible. He had the same idea, pressing me up against the back of the door. He cupped my jaw with both hands, helping himself to my lips.

We kissed again and again, never settling, never quenching our thirst. I reached for his tie, nimbly undoing the knot and pulling the thing loose. It fluttered to the floor, leaving his neck open for exploration.

He slipped a hand underneath my purse strap, depriving me of its weight. Setting the bag down on the credenza, he began undressing me. First it was my shoes. One by one, he helped me out of them, returning to my mouth a moment later. I was significantly shorter without my heels, and I had to tilt my head up to succumb to his kisses.

Next, he moved on to my dress, pushing the fabric off one shoulder so that he could access my skin. I countered his play by undoing his top button. Suddenly, I could see his Adam's apple, and the stubble from the razor that morning.

I left his mouth to kiss along his jaw line. Using my tongue, I explored the ridges and valleys of his neck. He was hot and growing hotter. I tasted aftershave and sweat, a combination that was intoxicating. He grew tired of focusing on a single shoulder, and reached down to grab a fistful of my skirt.

Peeling it up and over my head, he divested me of the only garment I wore. Tossing it over the sofa, he was careful not to hurt the fabric. So contentious, even in the throes of passion, I marveled at his self-restraint. I wanted to rip his shirt, to pop the buttons at his waist and shove his pants to the ground. Yet he was one step ahead of me, revealing my body before I could get my hands on him.

He picked me up, carrying me back to the guest bedroom. I wondered why we didn't go to his room, but realized there were probably stairs involved. The guest room was the closest mattress available and in his haste, he didn't consider anything else.

He laid me down, gentle and yet provocative. I reached up to gather him into my arms. This was everything I wanted and nothing I had expected. The previous night I lay awake in this very same bed, wondering if I would ever touch him again. It seems I had my answer.

He kicked off his shoes, joining me atop the mattress. I slid over to allow him room, turning toward him at the same time. He leaned over me, lowering his lips to mine. The kiss was soft and mysterious, just the tip of the iceberg with a mountain underneath.

I reached for the hem of his shirt, eager to dispense with the intrusive fabric. Pulling it up over his back, it reached only so far before getting caught on his ever-widening chest. He leaned back, undoing the buttons that held the thing in place. Ducking out of the attire, he dropped it onto the floor. It seemed that he had far less respect for his own clothes than he had for mine.

Excited, I pulled him back to me, sliding my hands up and down his spine. His form was a stroke of genius, a masterpiece that only I was privy to. It felt dangerous, even illicit, to allow myself the pleasure of his company. I was supposed to be hiding out. I was supposed to be afraid. And yet neither of those things were true.

I was there in the blessed moment, enjoying myself and allowing Nate to enjoy me as well. He sealed our kiss, dipping his head low to capture my earlobe. It was the most erotic thing I had ever experienced. The way he sucked on my flesh, turning it over underneath his tongue. Lightning bolts of pleasure shot through me, and I ached for more.

Sliding my arm around his shoulder, I hung on for dear life. He was on top of me, pressing me down into the mattress. I spread my legs, hungry for his love. After a heated moment, he left my ear and moved down my neck to my collar bone.

I ran my fingers through his hair, alight with curiosity. What new sensation would he introduce me to next? He seemed to be quite knowledgeable in the bedroom. I didn't want to think about all the women who preceded me, or anyone who might come after. For the time being, it was just me and Nate, alone and on fire.

I smoothed my fingers along the yolk of his shoulders, feeling the fine bone and muscle structure as they worked. He sucked a circle of skin into his mouth, and I nearly drowned from the pleasure. I knew that would leave a mark, and that I would have to hide it, but I didn't care.

He slid my bra straps down my arms, reaching behind me to undo the clasp. Freeing my breasts, he dangled the bra over the side of the bed, dropping it to gather dust along with his shirt. He took a moment to examine me, as if I were a gourmet meal or an expensive bottle of wine.

I looked up into his eyes, my heart racing, my breath caught in my throat. I waited for him to say something about my birthmark, but he didn't. Instead, he put a hand on my hip and lowered his mouth to my chest. I closed my eyes to concentrate on the sensations. He licked his way up one mound, circling the nipple with the tip of his tongue.

Back arching, I moaned. Every single movement was delicious torture. Every heated breath against my skin was another chance at redemption. I wondered how I had gotten so lucky. Surely there were more worthy women than I to share Nate's bed. He was a billionaire who rescued me from the gutter. He should be with an heiress, or a princess, or some other fabulously wealthy person.

I pushed those thoughts from my mind. For whatever reason, Nate chose me, and I was determined not to let him down. I wanted to play with him the way he was playing with me. There was only one way to get what I was after, and that was to assert myself dramatically.

I wrapped my legs around his waist and rolled to the right, pulling him along with me. Sitting up, I looked down at him in awe. He put his hands on my thighs, a picture of masculinity. I reached for his waistband, undoing the buttons and peeling the fabric away.

He knew where I was going, I could see it in his eyes. He wanted it just as badly as he wanted me. I picked up one of his hands and licked his index finger. Biting gently, I swirled my tongue around the tip. He grinned, ready for more.

I pushed his pants down, releasing his hand so that he could help me. Together, we made short work of two of the last remaining obstacles in our path: his pants and his underwear. I moved them to the side. Taking hold of his waist, I framed his massive manhood, examining it before beginning my descent.

He was at full attention, the swollen head pointed in my direction. I lowered myself onto my knees between his legs, inching down the mattress until my head was in the right position. Gripping the thing by the base, I guided it to my lips. Kissing softly at first, I began to lick from bottom to top like a giant lollipop.

He groaned, attempting to be patient while I teased him in the worst way possible. I leaned back and blew a stream of cold air onto his heated shaft, following it up with more gentle licks. I felt his abdominal muscles contract and expand, and I knew I was doing the right things.

Opening my mouth, I slid his tool all the way in, closing my lips around him.

Filling myself up with his rod, I sucked deeply, eliciting another moan from him. He put his hand on the back of my head, not holding me down, but just guiding me forward. After a long stretch just feeling him at the back of my throat, I began to move. Gliding up and down, I swallowed and then released him, urging him toward the promised goal.

Each time he split my tonsils, I relished his weight. And each time I pressed my lips to his head, I marveled at the smoothness of his helmet. Driving down again and again, I brought myself to the brink. I felt my inner landscape grow wet and hot with desire. He was all that I needed, and I had him right where I wanted him.

He urged me to move faster, and I obeyed, bobbing up and down like a sex toy. I almost brought myself to climax. Even without his meat between my thighs, the sensations were unworldly. I wanted him to cum, wanted to taste the salty spray and feel the satisfaction of a job well done. But he grasped me by the arms and lifted me up, detaching his cock from my lips.

I panted heavily, lusting after his unfinished business. He didn't pause in his quest, pushing me onto my hands and knees above the pillow. He pulled my underwear down, tossing it behind him as he got into position.

Standing on his knees behind me, he guided his flesh toward my opening. I felt the blunt end of his stick pressing against my flower. He circled my clit, egging me on, teasing me with the knowledge that I would soon be full.

I dug my fingers into the blankets, clawing my way to victory. He struck a moment later, digging himself in deep. One moment I was lonely and aching, and the next I was complete. I felt him enter as a wave of pressure washed over me, its triumph filling me and surrounding me at the same time.

He gripped my hips, thrusting himself into place. I moaned, tossing my head around. My hair bounced against my shoulders as he lunged forward and back, beating me into submission. I opened as wide as I could, leaning back into the onslaught. It felt so good. Every stroke was a masterpiece, every whack of my bare bottom a delight.

The tension dissolved within my core, as Nate planted a seed of new growth. He took me away to a better place, driving out the demons of fear and despair. I needed him to cum. I was fast approaching my own orgasm, and I wanted him to peak alongside me. I held on as long as I could, denying myself the one thing that my body screamed out for. But it was too late. I was already flying.

I felt myself leave my body, soaring high above the house, up into the stars. Nate had given me wings, and I used them to glide around paradise, learning all there was to know about life's magical moments. From way down on earth, I felt Nate plunge into me, beating his way toward conclusion. He paused a moment later, emptying his load, splitting me in two with his love.

I floated lazily back to reality, finding myself still crouched on the bed, Nate's dick between my legs. He lowered himself on top of me, exhausted and content. We fell down to the mattress together, nestling softly above the blankets.

He pulled me close, wrapping an arm around my chest. I lay there sleepily, enjoying the aftermath. This was where I belonged and I knew it. I was going to enjoy myself for as long as I was physically able to do so. It was wrong to fall in love with my boss, but we were past all that already. Nate was in my heart. He was in my mind, and he had been in my body.

I forgot all about Marcus and why I was supposed to be afraid. It didn't seem to matter what brought us together, only that we were joined in the same bedroom, in the same bed, in each other's arms. For the first time in a long time, I drifted off to sleep, knowing that I was safe. Nothing could hurt me as long as Nate was there. And I hoped he would always be there, as long as we both should live.

Chapter 25

Nate

I didn't have the vocabulary to tell Ava how I felt. I thought I said it pretty well with actions. I liked her a lot, I maybe even loved her. Not that I would say such a thing. Emotions weren't my strong suit, and I kept my heart well camouflaged behind layers of competence and business acumen.

She stayed with me for a week, and while I thought it was just the beginning of a long-term relationship, apparently she was just biding time. My mother showed up one afternoon to tell Ava that she found a new apartment.

I pulled the woman into my office to berate her. "Why would you tell her that?" I demanded.

"She deserves to know," Mom answered, looking shocked by my reaction. "I figured she might be looking for a place of her own by now."

"It didn't occur to you that I might enjoy having her live with me?" I snarled.

"I'm not talking about you," Mom replied, even tempered as always. "This is Ava's decision."

"If you didn't offer her a new apartment, she wouldn't have to choose," I said, regaining my composure.

"Then consider yourself lucky," Mom shot back. "If she wants to stay with you, you'll know."

I turned away. I didn't want to give Ava a choice. Did that make me a bastard? Thinking through it, I realized that I had to at least let her know that there was an apartment available. But I hoped she would decline the invitation.

To my shock and horror, she did not. She looked pleased that she would finally be able to get out on her own. I bit down on my bottom lip, feeling my control over the situation slip away. Why had my mother decided it was up to her to get involved? Why had Ava chosen to leave? I realized that I might be reading too much into it, but I couldn't help myself.

This was the first time in a long time that I felt a connection to another person. All the women before Ava had been one-night stands or friends with benefits. I didn't have what I considered to be a real relationship.

Maybe it was because of my father. Maybe it was because I saw the way things played out with my mother, and I learned that women were either sex objects or doormats. I didn't like to think of my mother that way, but that's what it seemed.

Ava was neither. She was a person I connected with, a strong and sensual creature that I wanted to keep by my side. It didn't occur to me that she might feel like she was putting me out. I was savvy enough to know when someone was using me for my money. It wasn't like that with Ava.

I smiled when she and my mother started talking about moving her things. I agreed to open up my house when they were ready, but I objected to lending a hand. I told them I was busy that day, that I had a meeting I couldn't get out of.

Ava looked up at me from her desk, a little bit hurt. I didn't know what was going through her mind, and I didn't want to guess. But gazing down at her, I thought I could see some pain in her eyes.

Turning around, I marched back into my office, shutting the door behind me. I couldn't deal with her feelings on top of my own. All my life I remained carefully aloof, doing my best not to get dragged down into a sticky love story. Yet here I was, deeply embroiled in the very thing I had hoped to avoid.

It was my own fault. I let myself fall for the woman. If I had kept my head clear, and kept my heart out of it, I wouldn't be in this mess. I could just watch her walk away and think nothing of it. But I took a chance and got comfortable. It was going to be my undoing, I was sure.

Ava wanted to move out as soon as possible. That was fine by me. I didn't think I could go to bed with her that night knowing that she would be vacating the home. I wanted to invite her to stay, to ask her why she thought she had to leave, but I couldn't find the words. My heart had been sure that she was the one, but apparently it was wrong. There was no way to reconstruct the good times after that. I needed to be alone to lick my wounds.

I drove Ava home that night because her car was at my place. Mariah met us at the front gate, and I let both women inside. I excused myself to go to my home office, pretending to have work to do. I actually did get a few things done. I answered some emails and took a call from some distributors in France.

By the time I was done, they were gone. Ava's car disappeared from my driveway, and her things vanished from my room. I wandered through the house, imagining her in the kitchen and in the living room. The closet in the guest room was still full of her dresses, and there were some other things remaining. I lingered with them, imagining Ava paging through the closet trying to figure out what to wear. I was going to drive myself crazy if I continued on in that fashion.

Texting Peter, I demanded that he meet me for a drink. It was stupid. I felt like I had been dumped. That wasn't at all what happened. Though we didn't talk about it, and I couldn't be sure. Being in a relationship was difficult, if we even were in a relationship. We hadn't even talked about that. I was out of my depth, wrapped up in my own delusions. If I thought I could just walk into domestic bliss, apparently I was mistaken.

Peter was a champ. He hadn't left the office yet, but agreed to meet me downtown. I staked out a spot at the bar and waited for him to join me. He didn't disappoint, swinging by after only a few minutes.

"What's up?" he asked, holding a hand out for the bartender.

The man walked down, providing Peter with a napkin. "What'll it be?"

"Scotch on the rocks."

The employee poured a glass and handed it over, accepting Peter's twenty. Making change, he walked away to provide for the next customer, leaving Peter and me alone. I finished the last of my own drink, bummed beyond my ability to conceal it.

"Ava moved out."

"I didn't realize she had moved in," Peter said.

"We've been staying together," I informed him.

"You kept it secret," Peter marveled. "Well done."

"Except it's over now," I said. "My mom got her a new apartment."

"Wait, your mom got her an apartment?" Peter asked, confused.

"It's a long story," I sighed. "She's got some trouble in her past."

"Oh." He quieted down, understanding. He had been around enough to know what my mom's side hustle was. That meant there was an ex-boyfriend in the picture, and that the breakup hadn't been clean. "Is she going to be okay?"

"I think so," I answered, feeling bad that I hadn't considered Ava's safety myself. Of course, she was going to another one of the nonprofit's apartments. This one had a doorman, and a few other safety features, according to my mom.

"Have you told her how you feel?" Peter asked.

I looked at him like he grew two heads. "No."

"You might want to consider using words instead of actions." He pumped his fist, making a lewd gesture.

I gave him a playful shove. It was good to talk, good to have another perspective. We shot the shit for about an hour before Peter had to go. By that time, I was a good three or four drinks in, and feeling comfortable. He tapped me on the shoulder.

"See you in the morning," he rasped, putting down his empty glass.

I stayed for another hour, until I was too drunk to drive home and had to text one of my staff members to come get me. He drove me home and caught a ride back to wherever he lived. It was times like these I was grateful for my fortune.

Chapter 26

Ava

I was happy to have reconnected with Ari. She helped me move my things to the new apartment. Nate disappeared into his home office as soon as he let me in the gate, which was odd. I couldn't tell what was going on with him.

He invited me into his home, and I thought things were going well. I wanted to talk about what we were doing and where the relationship was going, but every time I tried, he changed the subject. I wasn't sure if he had someone else in his life, or if he was just uncomfortable having meaningful discussions.

Either way, it left me unsure which way to turn. I didn't want to assume that I was there for the long run. He didn't ask me to move in officially. He didn't ask me anything officially. It was all very casual, and that was fine. I certainly didn't need another hot and heavy romance. Dealing with Marcus was enough, though that fire had cooled. Maybe I wasn't ready to get involved with anyone else, although it was disappointing that Nate didn't try to stop me from moving out.

Mariah offered me the new apartment, and I immediately considered Nate's feelings. He stood beside me, listening in as his mother extolled the virtues of the new place. I glanced up, curious to see how he would react. But his face was a mask of stone, telling me nothing.

I was on my own, and I made the decision I thought would benefit everyone. Accepting the invitation, I was distressed to see Nate walk back into his office and shut the door. He was infuriating. I couldn't tell what he was thinking or how he was feeling. If he didn't want me to leave, why didn't he just say something? I didn't want to live in his home for an indefinite period of time without knowing that he wanted me there. In the absence of knowledge, I was just feeling my way forward.

The new apartment was lovely. It was smaller than the last, but cleaner. The flooring was updated and the curtains were clean. The carpet was fresher and the appliances in the kitchen were much more modern. The layout was a little bit different. You had to go through the bedroom to get to the bathroom, and the kitchen was on the far wall instead of right as you walked in the door.

The nonprofit had equipped this apartment with toys and games just like the previous one. I thumbed through the paperbacks, noticing that some of the titles were new and some were classic. I didn't want to read, remembering all the fun I had at Nate's place. I didn't want to watch cheesy rom-coms or take a bath by myself.

I felt like I made a mistake, but I didn't know what to do to fix it. I didn't feel like I could avail myself of Nate's charity forever. He hadn't said anything about how long I was welcome in his home, and every time I tried to bring up the subject, he avoided it. So we were at an impasse.

I texted Ari, inviting her out for dinner. She agreed, and I was able to get out of my own space for a few hours. It was strange. At my first apartment, I was so happy to be by myself, throwing ice cream parties in front of the television and enjoying quiet evenings alone. Things had changed in the short week I spent with Nate. I wasn't satisfied by myself any longer.

Ari was great company. We talked about fashion and pets. Ari had two cats and was thinking about getting a third. She was single and didn't care if anybody knew it.

"I'm becoming an old cat lady already," she teased.

"You're not an old cat lady," I responded, picking at my meal. "You just have a few cats."

"But how many cats is too many?" she wondered. "Like, if I get another one, I'll have three. Does three cats make you a cat lady?"

"I'm not sure," I answered. "Definitely six is too many."

"What about four?"

"I think four might be pushing it," I said with a smile. It was a relief to be discussing something so meaningless. Although, if I mentioned that I thought her pets were meaningless, Ari would probably have a bone to pick. "But three is fine."

"Phew," she sat back, as if the problem had been solved and we could move on.

I laughed. But then at the end of the meal, I had to go home alone. I sat down in front of my new television to watch something. I needed to take my mind off my own problems, but found that nearly impossible. Every man on screen was Nate, and every woman was me. All the stupid miscommunications that they experienced only threw my own failures back in my face.

The cues fell flat, and the drama imploded, leaving me unsettled. I turned the television off and went to bed. In the morning, Nate was cold and standoffish. I did my best to act professional, even though I was hurt. He didn't invite me in for breakfast, and he didn't have much to say to me throughout the day.

I wondered if he was upset that I had moved out. If that was the case, why didn't he just say something? I was in the dark and doing the best I could with the information at hand. Yet, he seemed to think I was no longer interested in an intimate relationship. He went from kind and loving to cold and distant in a heartbeat.

He called me into his office in the morning to give me a list of things to work on. There was no friendly inflection in his voice, nothing to suggest that we were lovers. He finished his directions and turned me loose, apparently expecting me to go back to my desk and perform the tasks.

I opened my mouth. I was about to tell him off. How dare he treat me like this, when all I wanted to do was lie in his arms? I wasn't the one who drove a wedge between us. Was it my imagination, or did he take my moving out as some kind of criticism?

A thousand accusations thundered through my mind, leaving me dizzy and breathless. In the end, I shut my mouth and walked away. I decided that he just needed some space. Things weren't over between us; they were just getting started. He would see that I didn't mean any harm. We weren't husband and wife or even a legitimate couple yet. Surely the simple act of leaving his home wasn't going to end our romance before it even really got started.

I told myself this as I worked to accomplish all the things he asked me to do. In the evening, I let myself back into his office to ask if he needed anything else. I had my own car, and I wasn't going home with him, but it was strange. I became accustomed to riding in and out of work with him. Our domestic life had been wonderful while it lasted. There was no reason that we couldn't do something like that again if we wanted. I just didn't need the crisis with Marcus to push us together.

"Can I get you anything else before I leave?" I asked.

"No," he said, turning back to his phone call. "Thank you," he added as an afterthought.

"I have some things left at your place," I said timidly, wondering if I could come over that night.

Nate acted like he didn't hear me. He was so focused on whoever he was talking to, that it was like I didn't even exist. I decided I would swing by his place later. If we weren't together, I wasn't sure how late he would work. Maybe nine o'clock was a safe bet.

I drove over to the gated community around nine, and found it locked. I buzzed Nate's home, but no one answered. I texted him but he didn't respond. Feeling rejected, I turned around and drove away. The next day was Saturday. I tried calling him but he didn't pick up. I drove over to see him, but he didn't come to the gate. I attempted to reach out in every conceivable manner, but he just ghosted me. It felt wrong. I was scared and hurt and all the other negative emotions piled up into one.

To that unappetizing soup, I added one more foul ingredient: self-loathing. I should have known not to start a sexual relationship with my boss. It was one thing to fantasize, but another thing entirely to fall into his bed. It was my own fault. I had no one to blame but myself. And yet, I couldn't help feeling anger towards Nate at the same time.

Why couldn't he talk to me? What was wrong with his voice and his words that he couldn't communicate simple concepts to a woman he cared about. I knew he cared about me. I could see it in his eyes and feel it in his touch. But even after we shared the most intimate of kisses, he couldn't think of a better way to treat me. If I didn't need the job so much, I would quit. If I had anywhere else to go, I would go. I felt trapped, even more so than I had with Marcus. Nate made me feel like I was less than human, not even worthy of an explanation. I drove back to my apartment to sulk in peace.

Chapter 27

Nate

I was hungover when I got into work on Monday. I spent the weekend in Atlantic City, throwing the dice and trying to have a good time. I thought about bringing one of my many girlfriends, but when the time came to call them, I chickened out.

There was only one woman I really wanted to take, and that was Ava. Aside from her, everyone else would be found lacking. So I went by myself. I stayed in the penthouse suite, and signed myself up as a high roller. Dropping tens of thousands onto the craps tables, I allowed the hotel to wine and dine me.

It felt good to have servants at my beck and call. I woke up in the mornings and went to the buffet. Afterwards, I lounged in the hot tub, chatting up the ladies. I started drinking in the early afternoon, and by night time I was wasted.

My phone beeped, letting me know that Ava was calling. She was outside my place and wanted to come in. I ignored the request. There was too much I wanted to say to her and no way to communicate from the casino. She wouldn't understand. Hell, I didn't understand.

I was taking her moving out way too hard and I knew it. She didn't realize how much she meant to me because I never told her. The solution was obvious. I had to talk to her. But that was the one thing I couldn't do, so I drowned my sorrows in glass after glass of Scotch.

I dragged myself back to Boston in time for work on Monday. Expecting to see Ava, I promised myself I would tell her everything. I would open my heart and find the words, dammit. I wouldn't allow excuses to get in the way. But she wasn't at her desk.

I opened up my computer to check my emails. Instead of a text or a phone call or anything so personal, she sent an email from her work address to mine, explaining that she was sick. She had cc'd HR, letting me know that the communication was an official request for time off and not a personal favor. I hit *reply all*, and approved her request with a friendly note saying I hoped she felt better.

I got very little work done. Every time I tried, I ended up staring out into space. Peter came to find me, following up on last week's conversation. He took one look at me and closed the door, as if shielding me from the rest of the world.

"You look like death," he swore.

"Thanks?" I asked.

"It's not a compliment. What the hell is going on?"

"I told you, Ava moved out."

"Talk to her then, tell her how you feel," he insisted, pulling up a chair.

"I can't do that," I sighed.

"Why the hell not?"

"Because it's just not who I am."

"Well then change," he instructed.

"I can't change."

"Then you're doomed to sit here in the dark for the rest of your life." Peter rose, as if just noticing that the curtains were drawn. He pulled them back dramatically, flooding the office with light.

"Don't," I argued weakly.

"Get up man," Peter urged. "It's time for action."

I groaned. I didn't need this kind of pep talk. I was only interested in wallowing in my own misfortune. I lost a fortune in Atlantic City, and here, back home, I lost the only thing that really mattered to me, Ava's love.

I was a fool. I should have taken her in my arms way back when Mom offered her a new place. I should have told her that I wanted to stay, asked her if she wanted that too. Instead of standing by and watching her leave, I should have made my desires known. Maybe she was as confused as I was. Maybe she didn't know her own heart any better than I knew mine. If only I had given her a chance, rather than watching her walk away without putting up a fight. We could have been past all this drama already and on to the next fun thing. But because of my inability to express myself, we were stuck in two different rooms, each wondering what the other was thinking.

I got up, following Peter's direction. He was right; it was time for action. I sunk low enough on my own, it was time to face the music. One single conversation was all that stood between me and happiness. Surely, I could summon the courage to see it through.

A quick phone call to my mother netted me the address for Ava's new apartment. I used the pretense that she had called in sick for work and I wanted to make sure she was okay. It was a bit of a fib, but that didn't matter. There were perks to being a board member's son. I was determined to confess my feelings, to ask her to come back home with me and stay for a while. I didn't know what else I could offer, other than my heart. I knew she wasn't interested in my money, and that she was perfectly capable of taking care of herself. I only hoped I was enough, and that it wasn't already too late.

Chapter 28

Ava

I didn't have the courage to show up at the office. After stressing about it all weekend, I decided to call in sick. One day wouldn't make all my troubles magically disappear, but it might give me some added clarity. I just had to pretend that there was nothing wrong. It should be easy, just go into the office and do my job. I could be polite to Nate without offering him my heart. He made it clear that he wasn't interested in seeing me romantically.

In the meantime, I had a full day to myself in my new apartment. It wasn't exactly home, but it was mine for the time being. I examined the sofa and the television, wondering if there was a different way I could arrange them to suit me better.

A glass door led out to a balcony which allowed a lot of sunlight into the living room. The couch was turned away from the light, which I thought was poor conceptual planning. I struggled to turn the furniture, positioning it to take better advantage of the window. When I was done, I sat down to enjoy the fruits of my labor.

It was a little bit better. My heart wasn't really in it. I was hurt and it was hard to concentrate. I knew that I had to get over him, but the love that we shared wasn't easy to ignore. After a while, I became hungry. Since I had money in the bank, I could splurge and order delivery.

Astonished by the price tag, I nonetheless placed an order for a pizza. It wasn't every day that I sprang for delivery service, in fact, it was only about the third time I had done so in my life. But I felt bad, and it was a way to cheer myself up. Pulling the blanket off the bed and carrying it to the couch, I curled up to watch an old movie.

About a half hour later, there was a knock at the door. I thought it was my pizza. That was fast, and I was eager to sink my teeth into it. I already made up my mind to give the driver five stars for their quick turnaround.

Opening the door, my breath caught in my throat. It wasn't the delivery driver. The person standing in the hall didn't have a deli bag in his hands. It was Marcus, and he had a dozen roses. I slammed the door shut, but not before he grabbed the wooden surface, pushing it back. I felt the door bounce ineffectively off his palm, but I was already running.

There was nowhere in the apartment to get away. I lived there for all of one weekend and I already knew the floor plan by heart. There was the bedroom, that was it. That was the only refuge I had, other than the balcony.

If I chose the balcony, I would find myself two stories up, with nowhere to go but down. If I chose the bedroom, Marcus would make short work of the interior door and then we would be alone with only the bed between us.

I could run into the bathroom and corner myself in the shower, but what good would that do? No matter where I went, he would find me, and it would only be a matter of minutes. I cursed myself and my fate, turning around to face what was coming.

He stepped inside, grinning like a wild man. My heart leapt into my throat. Every fiber of my being screamed at me to run, but I forced myself to hold still. There wasn't anywhere to run. I had to confront the man and drive him out of my life. There was no one to help me and no possible way to call 911.

I glanced at my purse, all the way across the room on an end table. If I lunged for it to try to get my phone, he would see me. In a matter of seconds, he would snatch me up and pin me down, and I would be in worse shape than ever. So I froze, like a deer in the headlights, trying desperately to come up with a solution.

"You don't walk away from me," Marcus said, pointing a finger.

"You're the one who kicked me out," I replied, my eyes swinging around the room, searching for a weapon.

There was a lamp beside the couch. Or maybe I could make it to the hallway if I could coax him to the opposite side of the sofa. Thoughts were coming at me so fast, I could barely acknowledge them before another cropped up in its place. Why was he here? What did he hold against me? Why was he punishing me for his own transgression?

"I had a change of heart," he stated. "You didn't return my phone calls. You didn't thank me for the flowers."

"Thank you," I gulped. "They're beautiful."

"It's too late for that now," he snarled, hunting me down, forcing me back into a corner.

"Marcus," I tried, out of options.

"We could have been extraordinary together," he said. "But now I'll just have to settle for knowing no one else will have you."

He raised his arm above his head, the roses still grasped in his fist. I realized that he meant to beat me, to pound the stems into my face. It was a horrible way to go. Death by roses, not a girl's best friend. I put my hands up in self-defense, closing my eyes to the horror. There was a thud, and I thought I had been hit.

I slid my fingers over my forehead, searching for the debris or the blood that was surely evident. But there was nothing. A heartbeat later, the sound of a body collapsing close by prompted me to open my eyes. I saw Nate, standing in front of me, holding the lamp. On the floor between us, was Marcus' body. He was unconscious and sprawled out like an exhausted child, the roses crushed underneath one shoulder.

I couldn't breathe. The room began to sway. Every protective instinct I had told me to get away, to move past the person on the floor, to get some air. But when I put my hand out to steady myself, I felt my knees buckle.

Pitching forward, I lost all control. The world blacked out, leaving me with nothing but a ringing in my ears.

Chapter 29

Nate

I put the lamp down as Ava collapsed, rushing to her side. I stepped over the fallen attacker, catching her just before she hit her head on the windowsill. Her weight in my arms was familiar, and I was glad to hold her again, even though it wasn't in the best of circumstances.

My mind was racing. I arrived just in time to see this creep beat his way through Ava's door. She was backed into a corner of the living room, commanding all his attention while I snuck up behind him with the lamp.

All the boxing I had done did little to prepare me to bash someone's head in from behind. Instead of making a scene, or announcing my presence, I thought that finishing him off as quickly as possible was the best way to go.

I wasn't prepared for Ava to faint. She saw that I had arrived, and that she was no longer in danger, but that was the last conscious thought she had, it seemed. I reached for my phone to call

911, then picked her up and carried her to the couch.

Her ex-boyfriend stayed on the floor where he landed, not moving until the paramedics revived him. Ava herself woke up just a few minutes after she fainted, clinging to me as we sat, watching her attacker for signs of life.

"Nate?" she asked, her voice thick.

"It's okay," I responded. "I'm here."

"Where are we?"

"We're in your apartment."

"My apartment?" She put a hand to her forehead, sitting up to look around.

Startled by the sight of a man on her floor, she darted back into the safety of my embrace. I stroked her shoulder, telling her that she was safe without the awkward formality of words. There was a lot that needed to be said between us, but it was not the right time.

Thankfully, the police arrived quickly, and we spent the next hour dealing with the fallout. They handcuffed Marcus and led him off.

I didn't think to call my mother, but somehow, the leadership of the nonprofit figured out what was going on. One of the social workers arrived and talked at length to the first responders about the apartment and battered women in general.

A pizza delivery driver approached the open door, a pie in his hand. Ava stood up to thank him, transferring the box to the kitchen counter. She looked around as everyone wondered what she was doing.

"I ordered a pizza," she explained. "I thought Marcus was the delivery driver when he knocked, that's why I answered."

Everybody accepted her story, including me. I was amused when she opened the box and offered to feed everyone in the room. The two paramedics took her up on the offer, and the social worker elected to eat a slice. The policemen declined, leaving half a pie left over for Ava.

Finally, they all left and the apartment was ours once again. The social worker said that she would look into finding yet another place for Ava to stay, but I put my foot down.

"Give her some time," I interjected. "She'll let you know in the morning."

Ava regarded me with curiosity, keeping her pretty mouth shut until we had a chance to talk. I took her by the hands after locking the door, and led her back to the couch. Sitting down, we faced each other, as we should have done several days ago. I was the first one to speak. I had a lot to say, and no experience talking about my feelings. I put it off for too long, and it was time to come clean.

"I want you to stay with me," I said. "If you want to. That is, I'm inviting you to stay with me, as my girlfriend. Will you be my girlfriend? And move in with me?" It was choppy and ugly, but the words summed up my true feelings. I wasn't any kind of a poet. If that's what Ava was looking for, then I wasn't the right match. I didn't think she would care, as long as I wasn't keeping things from her anymore.

"Of course," she replied. "But why did you stop answering my calls?"

"It was stupid," I cursed myself for being so thickheaded. "When you moved out, I thought you didn't want to be with me anymore."

"That's not true. I didn't want to be a burden."

"You could never be a burden."

She looked pained and turned away from me. "You don't understand."

"No, I don't."

"When you have nothing, and you have to rely on the kindness of those around you, it can be easy to feel like a charity case. I am, in fact, a charity case."

"No, you're not. Not to me." I held her hand close to my heart, willing her to see herself through my eyes. "You are strong and independent, organized, competent."

"Is this a performance review?" she snapped, pulling her hand away.

"I'm sorry," I said quickly, calling her attention back. "I've never felt like this before. I've had relationships but they've been very superficial. I have friends and people I hook up with, but I've never been monogamous with anyone."

"Do you want to be monogamous?" she asked, turning my whole world upside down with that one question.

There was only one way out of the situation, and that was through it. I couldn't run from my own heart anymore. I had to face up to my emotions and own them if I was ever going to get the outcome I wanted.

"Yes. I only want you," I said, holding her gaze with my own.

She inhaled sharply, placing one hand on either side of my jaw. "I only want you too," she answered my admission with a kiss. And with those magic words, everything else fell into place. She didn't feel safe in the new apartment, and who could blame her? We packed up her things and drove back to my house, arriving home, at last, as an official couple.

Chapter 30

Ava

Two weeks later.

I slipped down into the fragrant bath waters in Nate's gigantic tub. It was a fixture in the corner of his upstairs bathroom, an exceptional piece made of ceramic and tile. The entire bathroom was a wonder. I lowered myself until only my head rested above the surface of the water, gazing out at the luxury around me.

The walls were a soft cream color, with golden sconces and dim lightbulbs that approximated candlelight. The toilet was hidden away in a separate room, and the shower stall was big enough to sleep in. I found a box of bath beads, probably left over from one of Nate's previous house guests. It was lilac scented, and made my skin glow. I couldn't believe how spectacular things had turned out, as soon as Nate confessed his true desires.

He was out with his friends on the golf course, and I was alone in his tub. I squished the soap bubbles in my hand, sending them flying off to the far wall. I was in love, and I didn't care who knew it. Although I hadn't told Nate yet, and that was a barrier to be surmounted.

After inviting me to stay with him, he said relatively little about his own wishes. I thought that once we were past the keeping secrets phase of our relationship, that words would flow more naturally, but that didn't seem to be the case. We made love in every different position, in the bathtub and in the living room, and yet still, he couldn't bring himself to say those three little words.

I didn't want to be the first one to break that silent streak. What if I put my feelings on display and he didn't reciprocate? I knew how he felt. I knew that he was in love with me, and yet I doubted his ability to say so.

For a billionaire CEO, Nate was remarkably shy. He kept his cards close to his vest when it came to affairs of the heart. I wanted to take the lead, to show him how things were done, but I too was afraid. I didn't want to dangle my declaration out there all on its own. I needed some way to break the ice.

Getting out of the bath, I toweled off. I decided to make a meal for him, so that he could return home after triumphantly scoring three under par, and find a magnificent dinner. There was some lamb in the refrigerator, along with zucchini and squash. I decided to sauté them all with a very little bit of butter and olive oil, and make a big, tossed salad.

When the meal was finished, I poured myself a glass of wine and sat down to wait. I didn't have to wait long. Nate arrived at almost exactly the same time I finished. He carried his golf bag, slinging it down to the floor beside the door. He took one look at the spread on the table and smiled.

"What's the occasion?" he asked.

"No occasion," I said, strolling up to him as if I owned the place.

I put my wine glass in his hand, and tilted it up with two fingers, encouraging him to drink. He followed my instructions, finishing the liquid in a single gulp. Setting the glass down on the table, he took me by the waist.

I felt a shock to my system as he pulled me close, clapping our chests together without warning. His heart beat against mine, proof of his feelings even if he couldn't bring himself to say it. I held myself back, straightening my shoulders in an attempt to maintain my dignity. He wasn't fooled.

He nipped at my chin, teasing a smile from me. I relaxed, throwing my arms around his neck. I didn't need to stand on ceremony. I knew he loved me. It was obvious in every move, and every smile that he bestowed upon me when he thought I wasn't looking. No one felt the way he did without being in love. I would worry about language later on. This night was a night for passion.

Nate scooped me up into his arms and walked toward the staircase.

"Dinner will get cold," I warned him.

"I don't care," he said. "That's what the microwave is for."

I laughed. He was so blunt when he wanted to be, so single minded in his focus. I held on as he mounted the stairs, marveling at his ability to carry me. I wasn't heavy, but I was a whole other person, and he walked as if he didn't feel the burden. Maybe that was the conclusion I was supposed to come to. I wasn't a burden; not to him.

He took a left at the top of the stairs, walking into the primary bedroom. The sheets were made up by the cleaning service, perfectly washed and tucked. Nate set me down, and together, we pulled the covers back, revealing the mattress in all its glory.

Having uncovered the site of our greatest achievement, I flew back into Nate's arms. His kiss was so tender, it melted all my resolve. I couldn't imagine anything so sweet and spicy at the same time. His touch lit a fire in my heart and made my entire body tingle.

I reached up to stroke his ears, taking each one between my thumb and forefingers to explore its ridges. He answered by sliding his palms around my neck, easing his way toward my bra straps.

I pulled back, eager to give him what he wanted. Slipping out of my shirt, I tossed it onto the lounge chair. Unlocking the clasp behind my back, I gently removed my bra. I was no longer self-conscious about my birthmark. We didn't have to have that conversation. He never mentioned it, and didn't shy away.

I made a move to help him out of his clothing, but he beat me to it. Sliding his polo up over his head, he tossed it on top of my shirt, creating an intermingled pile of clothing that would wait for us to return.

Stepping back into his arms, I was once again treated to the warmth of his touch. He circled me with forearms and biceps made of steel, the product of many hours spent in the gym each day. I kissed his shoulder, then his bicep, then his abdomen, working my way down to my knees.

Kneeling before him, I slid my fingers beneath his waistband. He allowed me to undo his fly, but before I could take him into my mouth as I planned, he pulled me back to my feet. Helping me onto the bed, he reached for the elastic of my pants. I eased them up over my hips and down past my ankles, kicking them to one side.

Nate and I were both fully nude, lying with our heads on the pillow. Surprising me with a move we hadn't tried before, he rose up and turned upside down. Facing my lady parts, he split my legs, wrapping his arms around them firmly. I felt gentle fingers at the opening to my cave, and the rush of excitement that came with wicked fantasies.

I looked over to see his hard rod dangling close to my cheek. All I had to do was reach out and pet it, guide it to my lips for a suck. I swirled my tongue around its tip, feeling the opposite happening on my inner walls. Nate was engaged in his own dirty work, teasing me as I worshiped him.

I was so focused on what I was doing, that I didn't feel time pass. Every lick was answered by a corresponding stroke, every kiss I visited on him was reciprocated. I sucked deeper and harder as he pushed faster and farther down into my secret realm. It was hot and nasty. We toyed with each other's lives, the tension building on itself until it was almost too late.

Nate pulled away seconds before I thundered into the breach. I cried out, desperate for relief. I wanted him there inside me, buried deep, pushing and pulling with all his might. For one heartbreaking moment, I was devoid of love, but then he found me again. His lips on mine, one hand on my breast, he was frenzied and uncontrollable.

All I could do was widen my legs around him, gathering him into me. He dropped my breast to press his cock to my opening. His other hand was crushed up against my side, his breath heavy in my ear. My eyes rolled back as he shoved his way inside. The size of his member far outweighed his fingers. The blood thundered through my veins, searching for an outlet, bringing a flush to my chest as it rose and fell.

We were locked together in an embrace that would last a lifetime. He rode me like a lover, like an intimate partner who knew all his secrets. I saw his emotions clearly as he reigned over me, his brow glistening with sweat. I knew I had him. No matter what he said or didn't say, I knew his heart was with me.

I felt myself falling. Gently at first, but then with exaggerated vigor, I plunged down the rabbit hole into pure bliss. Nate came a moment later, digging himself deep to launch his missile. I gripped his backside, planting him firmly inside me. We hung breathless, shaking, tense and knotted together for one fascinating instant. Then he relaxed and lowered himself to his elbows, kissing my nose in playful relief.

I looked up at him, grateful for everything he had done for me. Maybe tonight was the night. I would tell him that I loved him and ask if he loved me too. I knew the answer already, but I wanted to hear him say it. We were living together under the same roof. He built up his courage enough to ask me to stay, now all I required was one final admission. I resolved to say the "L-word" before the night was over.

This is the end of Ava and Nate's love story.

Want to go straight to reading the next love story in this series with Jonas and Mae?
The title of the book is: Deal with Mr. Cruel - An agreement with consequences

Now available on amazon.

Or would you like to read a free romance novel from me instead? Then click here: https://dl.bookfunnel.com/oe2w1m9zxx

A little note at the end

You will look for contraceptives in vain in this book. Why is that? The story takes place in your imagination and should give you a carefree time and carefree reading pleasure.
In this world, all billionaires have six-packs and are really good in bed. STDs don't exist in this world.

I really hope you enjoyed this story. If so, I would appreciate a short review on Amazon. As an indie author, I don't have the resources of a major publisher, so this is the way you would support me the most.

Sign up for my newsletter and receive a free romance novel:
https://dl.bookfunnel.com/oe2w1m9zxx

Printed in Great Britain
by Amazon